DIRTY
TRICKS

By John Seelye

The True Adventures of Huckleberry Finn
The Kid
Dirty Tricks

DIRTY TRICKS

Or,
NICK NOXIN'S
NATURAL NOBILITY

☞

John Seelye

Liveright   New York

Liveright, 386 Park Avenue South
New York, New York 10016

1.987654321

Library of Congress Catalog Card Number: 73-89217
ISBN: 0-87140-094-4

Manufactured in the United States of America

For
Uncle Sam

For
Uncle Kurt

Contents

CHAPTER I

The
Noxin Doctrine

"Out of my way, there, Nick Noxin!"

The boy to whom this rude command was addressed paid it no heed, but continued to trudge toward home with his satchel of school books slung over his shoulder, his eyes resolutely on the unpaved road which was his chosen pathway, the time of our story being before the days of asphalt and concrete.

"Dad drat you, Nick Noxin!"

This curse was hurled over the shoulder of a boy who swerved past Nick on a bright red wheel, his face glowing hotly.

"Next time," cried the bicyclist over his shoulder, his bell ringing savagely, "I'll run you down without stopping!"

At that moment the boy's front wheel twisted in a pocket of sand, and he was thrown with some force into a roadside ditch.

"Ow-wow!" he cried in anger and pain. "I'll get you for that, Nick Noxin!"

"You have been the victim of your own haste, Frank Farley," said Nick, pausing to contemplate the other boy's predicament.

"If you had got out of my way, it wouldn't have happened!" cried Frank, getting to his feet and examining his various contusions.

"This is a public thoroughfare, I believe," said Nick calmly, "maintained by public monies."

"My father pays more in taxes than your old man earns in a year," sneered Frank, climbing out of the ditch. "Say, look here! My new wheel is ruined!"

"So I see," said Nick. "Heh heh heh heh."

"I'll get you for this, you . . . you *grocersboy!*"

"What did you call me?" inquired Nick, picking up a sizable stone from the roadway.

"What . . . what's it to *you?*" asked the craven Frank, looking about as if for help, although plenty of stones yet remained in the road near his feet.

"It's nothing to me, Frank Farley," said Nick. "Sticks and stones may break my bones, but names will never hurt me." Puckering his lips in a cheerful whistle, Nick Noxin continued on down the dusty road, leaving Frank behind.

"Just you wait!" cried that unhappy individual. "You'll be sorry!"

"Perhaps," said Nick, without looking back, "but you're the one who's sorry now."

The two boys went their separate ways, Frank limping back toward town, pushing his now useless wheel. He was (as my young reader has perhaps gathered) the privileged son of Squire Alphonse Farley, the well-to-do owner of Farley Farms, an agricultural establishment of considerable size, located in the rural, Southern California community of Poco Lobo, as is our story. A boy who always had plenty in his pocket, though without any visible effort on his part to earn it through the customary chores carried out by others his age, Frank had inherited great expectations but little love of hard work from his father, the industrious but grasping Squire. A physical coward with the usual bullying ways of his breed, Frank exhorted loyalty from a few of his schoolmates through the power of his wealth, and had managed to gather a small band of obliging toadies who flew to obey his most petulant commands.

Nick Noxin was in all ways Frank's opposite number. Though indeed a grocersboy, and quick to respond to insult in that regard, Nick derived no shame from his humble but worthy station in life. His father, a disappointed lemon grower, had invested his surviving capital in a small plot of land in Poco Lobo, adjacent to the main highway between Los Angeles and Santa Barbara, and

there, with his own skillful, self-reliant hands, had assembled a home which served also as a grocery store and
gasoline station. Though a "going concern," Mr. Noxin's
modest emporium was not exactly a prosperous operation, and the groceryman depended upon the unpaid
assistance of his four sons, of whom Nick, though not
the oldest, was the most promising.

At the point in time at which our story begins, Poco
Lobo was a small, rural community, though it is now a
thriving suburb of metropolitan Los Angeles. The town
was populated mostly by independent farmers who kept
the humble Quaker faith, and who scraped a meager living by wresting crops from an arid soil, unrewarding
labor which enabled them to observe with ease the
estimable teachings of their religion concerning the un-
importance of worldly wealth and the value of plain
dress and spare diet.

Though such as Squire Farley (who, like the other
wealthy businessmen in Poco Lobo, was an Episcopalian)
managed to squeeze a sizable income from his large land
holdings, which were well-watered by an irrigation system that he shared with his less fortunate neighbors
so long as they were willing to pay exorbitant rates for
the privilege, the rest of the townsfolk were barely able
to survive, and most of them were in debt. The retail
establishments of Poco Lobo were correspondingly humble, in marked contrast to several wholesale houses
located near the Southern Pacific tracks, to whose owners
the local farmers were forced to sell their meager pro-

duce at prices advantageous to the buyer. Prosperous appearing also was the bank of Mr. Aeneas Briggs, who owned many of the buildings of which the downtown area consisted and held large mortgages on the remainder. Banker Briggs was also in the possession of numerous notes of indebtedness for funds extended to the local farmers, notes which he was apt to recall without notice, at a whim and for his own diversion, usually a week or so before harvesttime and at Christmas and the Fourth of July. Though Banker Briggs was not loved by his fellow townspeople, he was certainly feared, a species of regard which that elderly man of money seemed to prefer above all other.

The Noxin family did not labor, I am happy to say, under the onerous liability of a mortgage held by Banker Briggs. They were "free and clear," as the saying goes, thanks to Mr. Noxin's industry and a small legacy inherited by his wife at a convenient juncture. Moreover, the Noxins had before them daily the example of the greatest Quaker of them all, Benjamin Franklin, whose *Autobiography* emphasizes that poverty is no permanent condition in a new country, where thrift and hard work can bring prosperity and even worldly eminence to the lowliest American citizen, and the pages of which were employed as wallpaper in the Noxin home, serving the double purpose of decoration and education (insulation not being a necessity in Southern California), a use which the venerable Sage of Philadelphia would surely have approved.

Since he is the hero of our tale, let us follow Nick Noxin home, studying as we do so his face and figure, so revelatory of character. Even under the light powdering of dust, occasioned by the velocity of Frank Farley's passage, a careful student of physiognomy could have detected telltale signs of resolute character. Though slight and short of stature, Nick Noxin bore himself with manly dignity, and his dark features were gathered in a pleasant scowl under the black curls of his tousled head, a fixed and thoughtful expression of agreeable determination, given particular focus by his nose. Though his dark eyes were more narrow than wide, and rather close-set, they nonetheless conveyed the impression of an intelligent wariness, rather remarkable in one of his tender years, our hero being scarcely fourteen at the time of our story. Nick's appearance was further enhanced by his gait, which if slow was steady, as with each step his bare toes gripped the dirt of the road with sturdy purpose. Though his feet were somewhat splayed, their very flatness lent our hero an appearance of great stability.

Arriving home, Nick greeted his mother with an affectionate salute, placed his book satchel in his room, and joined his brothers at their common labors in their father's store. We now find them all hard at work, as their father worked the crank of the gasoline pump outside, filling the capacious tank of the Studebaker limousine owned by Banker Briggs.

Obie Noxin, the oldest brother, was busily unpacking cans of tomatoes, holding them back with one hand as he placed them on the plain board shelves which, despite Mr. Noxin's skill at carpentry, had somehow settled into an inconvenient tilt. But Obie had mastered the art of bracing the cans against one another so that, when he was finished, they would remain firmly in place until one was removed.

Hardy Noxin, two years younger than our hero, was industriously sweeping clouds of dust toward a swarm of flies buzzing about the twists of flypaper which dangled from a speckled ceiling, and little Knox Noxin, age five, was perched on a large rat cheese into which he was energetically boring holes with a screw auger. Half the wheel of cheese already resembled the product associated with the Alps and the yodel. A sign neatly labeled "SWISS" lay drying on the counter nearby, and on the same broad surface was spread a newspaper, over which was bent the sign painter, none other than our hero himself, who had seized a spare moment to inform himself on current events.

The proprietor of the store now entered, mopping his balding head with the clean portion of an oily rag. "Good work, Knox," said Mr. Noxin, using the selfsame rag to wipe the nearly completed cheese free of dust and parings. "It would fool a Dutchman."

"Father," said Nick, carefully refolding the newspaper and replacing it in a homemade, wooden rack which bore the carefully lettered legend "POCO LOBO HOWLER," making sure to brace the stand against the counter, thus counteracting its tendency to wobble,

"Would you be so kind as to explain to us again the principles behind which changing an ordinary rat cheese into a Swiss cheese is an act of philanthropy? I should dearly love to commit them to memory."

"Certainly," said Mr. Noxin, pulling out his golden Tiffany railroad watch and consulting it. "I see that it is only a few minutes until closing time, so we might as well devote the interval to edifying discourse." At this, his boys quickly found seats on the various boxes and barrels placed near the counter on which their father was leaning, for they all dearly loved to benefit from Mr. Noxin's wisdom, the carefully gathered hoard of forty-five years of Western life. Though he had never had the advantage of a university education, Mr. Noxin was not without learning in the way of the world, having, as he put it, attended the School of Hard Knocks in times past.

"To begin with," he said, "Honesty is the best policy. And what is Honesty? Honesty is giving a dollar's worth for a dollar tendered. Rat cheese normally sells for ten cents a pound, Swiss cheese for twenty cents a pound. We shall sell this cheese at ten cents a pound, guaranteeing the customer his money's worth." Pausing a moment to let his words sink in, Mr. Noxin took out his pocket-knife and thriftily carved a toothpick from the store counter, which he placed in his mouth. "Now," he went on, "a satisfied customer is one who is sure he has received his money's worth, and therefore a customer who thinks he has received more than his money's worth is *more* than satisfied. He is *pleased.* And it is my privilege to share his pleasure, without expending more than a few idle moments with a screw auger and pen. Now, Nick, will thee * explain to us the true meaning of Philanthropy?"

"I shall be glad to, Father," said our hero, springing from his cracker barrel and assuming the classic orator's stance taught him by Mr. Cosmo Castle, A.B., one foot held six inches behind the other and a finger pointed straight upward, leaving one hand free to move about in dramatic accompaniment to his words. "Philanthropy," said Nick with a flourish, "is the love of mankind. One loves mankind so that one in turn will be loved by mankind. One does unto another more than the other expects will be done unto him so that he will reap the profits therefrom, a triple profit if what is done unto another involves no extra cost to oneself."

"Thus," concluded Mr. Noxin, "to sell rat cheese as Swiss cheese but at rat-cheese prices is to profit in proportion to the extent that the customer is pleased by the prospect of buying Swiss cheese at rat-cheese prices. It is philanthropy, because it enables many who would not ordinarily be able to afford Swiss cheese to buy an article acceptable *as* Swiss cheese, but without extra cost, an article which those who can afford Swiss cheese would not buy anyway, not deriving any pleasure from purchasing what they assume to be less in quality than the

---

* Mr. Noxin, it will be observed, affected the picturesque Quaker "plain speech" while in the bosom of his family.

article which they can ordinarily afford at regular prices. It benefits the poor and solaces the rich. It earns us the gratitude of the former, but does not bring upon us the enmity of the latter. It does great good and no harm."

"Indeed, Father," chimed in Nick, "selling rat cheese as Swiss cheese but at rat-cheese prices is a truly Christian act, worthy of Him who turned water into wine."

"Thee speaks like thy father's son," said Mr. Noxin, "and thee deserves a fitting reward."

Taking out his pocketknife, Mr. Noxin sliced off a morsel from the rat cheese in question, which he handed to his son.

Nick took his reward and nibbled at it solemnly for a moment, his face taking on its customary dark hues of reflection. "This is," he said, "as good a piece of Swiss cheese as I have ever eaten."

"Spoken like a true Noxin!" cried his father. "I think I'll have a slice myself."

CHAPTER II

A Conversation on the Porch

☞

Later that evening, having shared with his wife and sons a frugal but hardy repast of wieners and beans, Mr. Noxin seated himself on the front porch of the small but sturdy house which he had built with lumber especially selected by him from the numerous crates and boxes cast aside by the wasteful warehousemen down by the tracks.

Seated in a chair cleverly constructed from an orange crate, Mr. Noxin carefully opened the evening paper just as a nearby streetlamp turned on, and in the glow thus provided, began to read. In order to instruct his boys in healthy and saving ways, Mr. Noxin illuminated his home by available light, including the sun and the neighboring streetlamp, the proximity of which he had reckoned on in constructing his modest domicile. This was but one of the many small economies which the Noxin family practiced in order to make ends meet.

A short while later there came a thump and a groan from within the darkened house, followed by the squeak of hinges as Nick opened the screen door and closed it softly after him, joining his father on the porch. "Mother has been rearranging the furniture again," our hero observed, examining his shin in the light from the street-lamp.

"It is a harmless pastime," observed his father, "and one which prepares us for the prevalence of unexpected obstacles to our progress in this world."

Since his father continued to remain absorbed in the newspaper, Nick seated himself on the porch railing, catching hold of the supporting post as his perch shifted under this weight. For the next half hour he amused himself cheaply but pleasurably by observing the various insects, one of the many resources with which Southern California is amply endowed, as they swarmed about the yellow globe of the nearby streetlamp, and by sniffing the nighttime air, which was filled with fragrance from the blossoms of the nearby citrus groves.

Thus had Mr. Noxin instructed his sons in the enjoyment of the simple and virtuous pleasures of rural life, thereby avoiding the snares and delusions of artificial pastimes, such as Chinese checkers, Parcheesi, and jigsaw puzzles, those consummate time-wasters so often seductive to American boys. "I fail," he said in regard to such games, "to see the profit in them. All play and no pay makes Jack a poor boy."

Our hero was eventually joined in his pleasant recreation by his father, who beforehand had carefully refolded the evening paper and set it aside, so that it could be placed with the other unsold papers and returned to the news agent the next day. Having several times taken in deep breaths of the sweetly scented air and expelled them with sounds of gratification, Mr. Noxin turned to his son.

"A penny for thy thought, Nick," he said, without, however, proffering the coin in question.

"I was thinking, Father," said Nick, "that the insects which flutter about our streetlamp are like those people who are attracted to cheap fame and easy riches, lures often as fatal as they are illusory."

"Well put," said his father. "Thee has a talent for fresh and vivid images, apt analogies remarkable for one of thy tender years."

"Thank you, Father," said Nick. "Dr. Cosmo Castle has been so kind as to make a similar observation upon occasion."

"Professor Castle informs me that thee takes naturally to the forensic arts," said Mr. Noxin. "He predicts that thee will go far if thee enters a profession in which persuasion figures largely."

"He has said much the same to me," said Nick, modestly.

"Which reminds me," said Mr. Noxin, "that I have

been meaning for some time now to discuss the subject
of thy future, son." Carving a splinter from the porch
rail, he placed it thoughtfully in his mouth. "Though
thee is yet young, it is never too early to consider such
matters."

"I should very much appreciate the opportunity to
benefit from your counsel in the important matter of my
chosen profession," said Nick. "Especially since I shall
be entering high school in the fall."

"Whatever pathway through life thee happens to
choose," said Mr. Noxin, "I hope that thee never looks
with disdain on those callings which, though perhaps
lowly in themselves, are vital to the well-being and continued growth of our national economy. Without the
simple but honorable skills of those who wield the jack-
hammer and rivet gun, the inventions of intellect would
be but airy fancies."

"You need not fear that the son of Norman O. Noxin
will ever lose sight of the proper relations of things,"
said Nick. "America was built by the hewers of wood
and the drawers of water. The smooth hand that guides
our nation's finances is dependent upon the calloused
hand in the till."

"Well said," said Mr. Noxin, examining his own
fingers as he dislodged a bit of axle grease from under a
thumbnail with the aid of his toothpick. "Though our
heads may be in the clouds, let us not forget that our
feet are on the ground, nor let us disremember the
sacred text which reminds us that our bread will be

earned by the sweat of our faces. Has it not been written, 'The meek shall inherit the earth'? (Matthew 5:3). Which I interpret as meaning that the *earth* is not merely the *inheritance,* but the *portion* of the Meek, thereof."

"The fifth chapter of Matthew has always been dearest to my heart, Father," said Nick, reverentially. "Indeed, I value our present humble condition because of the meekness it naturally engenders, and the love of peace which necessarily follows, and pray that I may remain lowly at heart and peaceably inclined though lifted to whatever position of eminence the Good Lord intends for his humble servant, for humility is ever the touchstone of virtue, once lost, seldom to be regained."

"Humble origins and great attainments," said Mr. Noxin, "are not the exception but the rule in this great land of opportunity. Indeed, lowly beginnings and a modest demeanor are valuable assets in a country claiming the birthplace of Abraham Lincoln and Thomas Alva Edison, to say nothing of Benjamin Franklin, Andrew Carnegie, and Horatio Alger."

"As you know, Father," said Nick, "the history of our country and the biographies of her great sons have ever been my study, that streetlamp and these humble floorboards my substitute for firelight and ash shovel. Only the other day I walked through the broiling midday sun to claim a nickel that our saintly but otherworldly mother was overcharged by the clerk at Thatcher's Drygoods Emporium, an act that did not go unobserved by Mr. Phineas T. Thatcher, himself."

"Only a distinguished military record," observed Mr. Noxin, "lays a firmer foundation than poverty for a rising edifice of fame in America, and, combined, they are unbeatable."

"I do hope," said Nick, "that when the call to serve my country in time of war is sounded, that I shall not be behindhand in responding."

"I am sure that thee shan't," said Mr. Noxin. "And now, Nick, what profession, in particular, does thee have in mind?"

"In my study of national history," said Nick thoughtfully, "particularly through that volume entitled *Famous Firsts* which you gave my brothers and me for Christmas —the factual material in which is amusingly and instructively interspersed with advertisements for various patent medicines distributed by a Chicago wholesale firm—I have determined that the most telling events in the record of humanity's struggle upward are often enough the creation of statesmen and legislators, and that the surest road to the chambers of political power is paved by the study of Law."

"Excellently observed," said his father. "Of course, my opinions regarding the profession of Law have always been mixed. Though some lawyers are men of probity and virtue, many are not, and use their arcane knowledge of the twistings and turnings of legal niceties for wicked ends. I know whereof I speak."

"You have often mentioned the difficulties attendant upon the probating of Mother's legacy," said Nick, "but

I should sincerely hope that if good fortune so directs my steps toward the profession of Law, that I shall remain loyal to the honest scruples of our faith."

"I am sure that thee will," Mr. Noxin hastened to reply. "I only meant that it is a path beset with many temptations."

"Indeed," said Nick, "one of my purposes in considering the profession of Law is my desire to drive out the wicked from their ill-gained seats of power. I came to this resolve by reading of the Teapot Dome scandal, in which so many reputations, until now thought stainless, have been stripped of gaudy pretense, and shown to be smirched with the black pitch of corruption."

"By Jehu!" cried his father, uttering one of the few harmless expletives he allowed himself, and striking a calloused fist into a work-hardened palm. "Those rascals should be hung from their own oil derricks! They should be searched out and exposed to the unmerciful light of day, so as to vindicate the common man's faith in the basic purity of the capitalist system of free enterprise!"

Mr. Noxin warmed quickly to his subject, for it was one close to his heart. In selecting an advantageous location for his gas station, he had turned down the offer of another property as being too remote from vehicular traffic, land on which oil had recently been discovered. Moreover, as a dealer in petroleum and other oil-based products, including a number of patent medicines, he felt particularly well qualified to speak on the topic of California oil lands, and their unscrupulous leasing by

government officials to favored entrepreneurs without
the disadvantages of open bidding.

"Thee knows," he said to Nick, "how my blood boils
at the thought of competing in a market dominated by
favoritism and bribery."

"I have often heard you enlarge eloquently on that
issue," said his son, "and it was your indignation which
has lighted my way to the most important decision in my
young life."

"It is not that I am bitter over our own unfavorable
turn of fortune," continued Mr. Noxin. "Indeed, we
may yet have occasion to praise God for keeping us in
our lowly path of virtue and hard work, and I again cite
Chapter Five of the Gospel according to Saint Matthew. Had we purchased the other lot, thee and thy
brothers would by now be imperiled by the many temptations made possible by sudden and unearned riches."

"Oil encountered on the pathway of life makes for a
treacherous foothold," observed Nick sagely.

"Well put," said his father. "We might now be dwell-
ing in the mansions of the rich rather than the humble
cottages of the poor, our bodies clothed in silken rai-
ment, yea, and our home illumined by electricity and
staffed by idle servants with itching fingers."

"Verily," said Nick, "and clothed doubtlessly in the
gilt-encrusted livery modeled after the useless, antique
frippery of palace domestics, like that which makes such
a silly display of ostentation along Fifth Avenue, as we
have seen in the Rotogravure."

"Thank the Lord for the public prints," said his father. "For it is the newspaper which daily reminds us that gold is a snare and a delusion, and that its blinding glare has lured many honest men to their destruction. Thank God, I say, for Hearst!"

"Amen," said Nick. "I have often thought, Father, that the middle way is the best way, that enough is as good as a feast."

"Well said," said his father. "Such simple wisdom well suits thee. It is the homespun of honest reflection."

"After all," said Nick, "what is better than humble but virtuous labor? It is a thorny, obscure, and narrow path, but far better is it than the broad highway which easy success smooths for the unwary."

"Yes, indeed," said his father. "If thee bear such truths in mind as thee makes thy way through the world, I shall have no doubts concerning thy chosen profession. Indeed, Nick, I can hardly wait until thee has crushed the necks of the wicked oil interests under the heel of all righteousness, armed with just laws, perhaps written by thyself, and empowered with the authority of an instrument no less powerful than the Constitution itself."

"And what instrument is that, Father?"

"Why," said Mr. Noxin. "The Constitution itself, of course!"

"Daniel Webster," responded Nick, drawing on his deep fund of historical knowledge.

"Yes," said his father. "May thee cut the fabric of thy career to his pattern, Nick, and always remain an uncompromising foe of unrighteousness, never faltering in thy determination to do good in this world, at whatever cost to thy esteem in the eyes of the populace. Though, may it be said, Doing Good seldom lowers one in the estimation of one's fellowman, unless, of course, it be misapprehended as Doing Wrong."

"I shall always strive to be apprehended as Doing Good," said our hero soberly.

"Keep that sacred text before thee," said his father, "that tells us that 'Man looketh on the outward appearance' (I Samuel 16:7), nor neglect the wisdom of Paul, who wrote, saying, 'Abstain from all appearance of evil' (I Thessalonians 5:22). No less than the greatest Quaker of them all, Benjamin Franklin, heeded that advice, and made his way into the counsels of the great. You see, Nick," continued Mr. Noxin, warming to his subject, "we Friends strive always to appear virtuous in the eyes of men, for all the good intentions in the world, without approval, are as so much useless dust. Select thy associates wisely, in this regard, for by our acquaintance are we known. Recollect what thee has learned in the grocery business, Nick, and regularly attend to the culling out of the rotten apples, lest the whole bushel be spoiled. Remember, also, that stinking meats have their uses. What sauce can't save, throw in the paths of barking dogs, who will be distracted thereby from pursuing thee further."

"I shall not forget," said the dutiful son of N. O. Noxin.

"Yes," said his father, "as Daniel Webster tells us, 'There is always room at the top,' but he who gains it catches the rays of the rising and the setting sun, and is therefore more visible than the many at the base of the pile. Be not niggardly with thy associations, Nick, lest thee be caught shorthanded in matters of blame, but never choose those who seek the top themselves, lest thee find thyself suddenly cast into the shadow."

After exchanging mutual statements of regard and affection, father and son stumbled toward bed in the darkness of the Noxin home, leaving the night to the insects who continued their futile courtship of the seductive light cast by the streetlamp, which grew perceptibly dimmer during the long hours of early morning, as the pressure was lowered in the gas works many miles away.

CHAPTER III

A
Golden Opportunity
for the
Right Person

☞

When next we encounter our hero, Nick Noxin, it is early summer, and the approaching vacation from school has turned his thoughts to more remunerative employment than the chores of his father's store. Seizing a quiet hour, Nick was seated upon his favorite cracker barrel, devouring the contents of a recent number of the Los Angeles *Times* which he had found in a trash can on his way home from school. Such rich diet was a welcome relief from the spare contents of the *Howler*, which was devoted largely to local events.

Nick's quick eyes soon spotted a boxed item placed between the regular columns of advertisements:

BOY WANTED [*it read*]: THE TIMES IS SEEKING A YOUNG MAN OF DEPENDABLE AND REGULAR

HABITS FOR THE POSITION OF OFFICE BOY. A FINE OPPORTUNITY TO LEARN AN HONOR- ABLE PROFESSION FROM THE GROUND UP FOR THE RIGHT PERSON. NOT A TEMPORARY POSITION. SERIOUS APPLICANTS CONSIDERED ONLY. NO STUDENTS, MEXICAN-AMERICANS, OR PERSONS OF COLOR NEED APPLY. ADDRESS INQUIRIES AND REFERENCES TO EDITORIAL OFFICES, TIMES BLDG.

His pulse quickening, Nick carefully folded the news- paper to the page bearing the advertisement, and ap- proached his father. Mr. Noxin was engaged in a delicate operation reserved for his hands alone. With a wooden scoop, he was mixing a quantity of fine white sand into the contents of a barrel marked "SUGAR." It was Mr. Noxin's theory that because of the well-known deteriorat- ing effects of sugar upon teeth, the introduction of a proportionate amount of abrasive would counteract decay through regular polishing. Thus, according to his calcu- lations, his customers were at no cost to themselves provided with an extra service, thereby saving the ex- pense of untold dentist bills. As we have seen, such small, unadvertised improvements formed the basis of Mr. Noxin's enlightened mercantile philosophy. Long before the harmful effects of rich dairy foods were detected by medical science, Mr. Noxin had saved untold lives from fatty degeneration of heart tissues by adding a quantity of water to his milk, and by mixing a substance in with his butter which, though based on a secret formula of his own, was (I can assure my young reader) without doubt made up of a large amount of vegetable oil.

"Father," said Nick, as soon as his parent had finished the improvement of his sugar, "I have been turning my thoughts recently to the subject of summertime employment."

"That reminds me," said Mr. Noxin, taking a crumpled handbill from his worn overalls pocket. "They are handing these out down at the post office."

WANTED! [*read the handbill*] BEANPICKERS! GENEROUS REWARDS FOR PIECEWORK! TEN CENTS A BUSHEL! WORK FOR ALL! APPLY IN PERSON TO MR. SNAGG, FARLEY FARMS. MEXICAN-AMERICANS, PERSONS OF COLOR AND STUDENTS ESPECIALLY URGED TO TAKE ADVANTAGE OF THIS OPPORTUNITY TO EARN BIG WAGES AT HEALTHY, OUTDOOR, TEMPORARY WORK. NO REFERENCES OR EXPERIENCE REQUIRED. LIVING QUARTERS PROVIDED AT REASONABLE RATES. BRING THE WHOLE FAMILY! A DANDY WAY TO SPEND YOUR VACATION WHILE EARNING A FEW EXTRA DOLLARS! ON THE JOB TRAINING. COMPANY STORE MAINTAINED ON PREMISES. COME ONE, COME ALL! PASS THIS ANNOUNCEMENT ON TO YOUR FRIENDS. THEY WILL BLESS YOU FOR IT. HELP BUILD AMERICA: PICK BEANS!

There followed an approximate translation in colloquial Spanish.

"Yes," said Nick, folding the handbill in neat fours, "but I had thought possibly of pursuing an occupation more congenial to my talents and aspirations than mere stoop labor." Holding out the newspaper for his father to read, he pointed to the advertisement. "I believe," said Nick, "that such work would not only pay more than picking beans, but would be highly educational, as well. As you have often remarked, our basic American liberties are dependent upon a free press and an informed public, and every concerned citizen should seize whatever opportunity comes his way to acquaint himself with the process by which raw events are converted to palatable accountings of fact."

"Well put," said Mr. Noxin. "I have always held the members of the Fourth Estate in high esteem, and have no objections to thy associating with such an honorable and useful calling, one which is forever linked to the name of the greatest Quaker of them all, Benjamin Franklin. As I have observed, a free press is as necessary to the American way of life as is the legislative process, for the one informs us so that we may duly exercise our liberties, as the other, by acting out the principles of the Constitution—maintaining their strength and vitality through frequent exercise—guarantees their perpetuity."

"As we have recently seen," said Nick, "the public prints aid in the uncovering of graft and corruption as the Law is instrumental in their persecution."

"Prosecution," gently corrected his father. "Yes, it is a truth that cannot too often be repeated: The Press and the Law are the right hand and the left of the Public Morality."

"I cannot wait to begin uncovering corruption!" cried Nick, and that very evening, laboring under the light of the streetlamp, he composed a letter of inquiry to the *Times*. After an hour of hard work and occasional consultations with his father, he wrote a final draft of his composition on a sheet of lined, yellow paper, which I print below verbatim as a model of its kind:

To the Editor of the Times:

Dear Sir:

I have seen in your informative columns, to which I am a regular subscriber, an advertisement seeking a young man of regular habits and native American origins for the position of office boy. It has long been my ambition to become a newspaperman, to assist in the promulgation of the information necessary for the maintenance of our American way of life, and I regard the opportunity you are extending to some fortunate youth as an excellent beginning to such a career. As I write this letter, I think of those mighty exemplars of the Fourth Estate, Pulitzer, Patterson, McCormick, and Hearst, and am eager to take the first step toward a profession which, even in the humblest hamlet of this great nation, executes the vital function guaranteed by the First Amendment to the Constitution of the U.S. of A.

I am asking that a reference be provided by Mr. J. Adams Quincy, A.M., my Grammar School Principal.

Very sincerely yours,
Nicholas Noxin

That night, I must confess, our young hero did not sleep as soundly as usual, for his dreams were crowded with excited visions of a summer spent in the daily turmoil of a metropolitan newspaper. The next morning, rising early and bolting down a quick but hearty breakfast of water gruel, a tasty compound of potatoes, turnips, and cabbages devised by Mr. Noxin and improved on considerably by his wife over the years, Nick ran all the way to school so as to encounter Mr. Quincy before classes began.

Nick found that dedicated pedagogue in his office, removing the faded blue overalls in which the principal addressed himself to his first duties of the day, namely, sweeping out the classrooms and raising the American flag on the pole outside. Poco Lobo, as I have already suggested, was not a wealthy community, and the principal was expected to execute chores not ordinarily associated with his exalted position. Not at all embarrassed by the unannounced arrival of Nick in his doorway, Mr. Quincy hung the overalls on a nail in his closet, and donned in its place the coat to the threadbare suit in which he daily ruled his educational establishment.

"Good morning, Nick," he said in the stern but not

unfriendly voice in which he habitually addressed his students. "You are early this morning."

"Yes, sir," said Nick, with a small bow. "I have a request to make of you."

"I see," said the principal, seating himself in the swivel chair behind his desk and motioning Nick to another chair, with a broken cane seat, that was placed to one side. "And what is that?"

Nick explained his errand, and gave both his letter and the advertisement to the principal, which that gentleman read with interest. "This *is* news," he said, leaning back in his swivel chair with caution, for the spring was broken and he had occasion from time to time to regret any precipitous movement. "Mr. Castle has informed me that you had chosen the Law as your future profession. In any event, I had assumed that you would be going on to High School."

"At my tender age," explained Nick, "it is foolhardy to be absolute in any such convictions."

"So I thought at the time," said Mr. Quincy. "But in this letter you seem to be quite definite in your plans for a career in journalism. Surely you are not thinking of leaving school without completing your secondary school education?"

"Again," said Nick, "it is my philosophy that one should remain flexible in all such matters. I don't know what my future holds, and it would be foolhardy to discount any opportunity which offers itself for promising and remunerative employment."

"I quite understand," said Mr. Quincy. "But you *say* that you plan to become a newspaperman. Is that not a shade dishonest?"

Nick blushed visibly. "Perhaps, sir," he said quietly, a dark frown gathering on his brow, "you are unwilling to provide the letter which I need in order to qualify for this position. In which case, I shall withdraw my request and seek elsewhere."

"You misunderstand me," said Mr. Quincy. "I have no objections to writing a letter praising your achievements. I was merely curious regarding your ultimate intentions as stated in this letter. If you do indeed intend to apply for a permanent position with the newspaper, though I regret your decision concerning High School, I shall be glad to provide the letter which you have requested."

"Let me put it this way," said Nick with an expressive gesture. "When I say that I plan to become a newspaperman, you may take it on faith that I plan at this point in time to become a newspaperman, whatever other plans I may have had at other times or will have in the future. Moreover, at the present time, I fully intend to pursue the profession of journalism with all the dedication that one would wish from an ambitious youth who intends to make that calling his career."

"I see," said Mr. Quincy, "that you are an apt pupil of Mr. Castle. But your cleverness at rhetorical evasions notwithstanding, it is clear to me that whatever your ultimate intentions may be (and I am more certain than

ever they will involve the Law), that they do not now
involve permanent employment by the Los Angeles
Times. Therefore, I cannot see my way clear to writing
the recommendation."

"You realize, of course," said Nick, "that without it
I shall probably not get the job, which means I shall
have to pick beans?"

Mr. Quincy shrugged. "You mentioned seeking references elsewhere, I believe," he said, rising and pinning a
policeman's badge to his worn jacket. "And now, Nick,
you must excuse me. The children will be arriving
shortly." From the closet Mr. Quincy took his policeman's
hat and white gloves, and headed for the door.

"I don't think you understand," said Nick. "We
Noxins . . ."

"On the contrary," said Mr. Quincy with a smile.
"I quite understand, and I wish you all the success you
deserve."

Without engaging in further pleasantries, the pedagogue left Nick alone in his office, and a minute later
our hero could see him at work outside, guarding his
pupils through the pedestrian crossing. Nick glared an-
grily at Mr. Quincy through the window, and made a
hostile motion with his expressive fist, entertaining
thoughts which I need not describe to my young reader.
In Mr. Quincy's defense it must be said that he was a
native son of New England, which accounted for his
severely stiff sense of correctness. This explanation, I am
afraid, was of no account to our hero, who had been

raised in the more generous traditions of the West, where a helping hand is ever the rule.

In accord with those traditions, also, Nick did not allow his destiny to be controlled by the refusal of another to lend a hand, and turned his own to the matter in question. His quick eyes noticed several sheets of the school stationery lying on the principal's desk, and nearby lay the stamp with which Mr. Quincy signed the routine correspondence of the day's routines: permission slips and the like. The ingenious mind of our hero went swiftly to work, and he followed, himself, soon after.

Shutting the door and seating himself at Mr. Quincy's typewriter, Nick ran a sheet of stationery embossed with the legend "Collis P. Huntington Memorial Grammar School, Poco Lobo, California: J. Adams Quincy, Principal" into the antique machine and carefully typed the following letter, also a model of its kind:

To the Editor of the Times:
Dear Sir:

I recommend to you for the position of office boy my star pupil, Master Nicholas Noxin, who shows promise of becoming a newspaperman of the stature of Pulitzer, Patterson, McCormick, and Hearst. He is sure to be a credit to your worthy journal, and I hasten to urge you to hire him at once and at as handsome a salary as his abilities and duties warrant.

> Very sincerely yours,
> J. Adams Quincy
> Principal

Cleverly placing the stamped signature of Mr. Quincy
on the letter, our hero slipped it into an envelope which
(I neglected to mention) he had already addressed on the
typewriter.

"There," said Nick with an alert glance out the window. "If I had more time, I could do fuller justice to
myself, but this is adequate for the purpose. It is less
than he should have said, of course, but certainly the
least he could do, considering my academic record and
the importance of this opportunity to my future."

The necessary letter now in hand, Nick was more
tolerant toward the principal, and a smile lightened his
features as he stood once more watching Mr. Quincy at
the crossing. "These pedants," he mused, for he was in a
quieter, contemplative mood following his recent crisis,
"do not understand the world of reality, sheltered as
they are in their academic heavens, and never having to
meet a payroll."

This last, perhaps I should explain, was one of Mr.
Noxin's favorite expressions, which he invariably used
when he wished, in his words, "to put things in their
proper perspective."

"It was," continued Nick to himself, "Mr. Quincy's
duty to write this note, and since he refused to do it,
someone else must do it for him." Adding further refinements to this logical syllogism, our hero opened the door
and left the office.

"Ah, there you are, Nicholas!" said Miss Tulips, his

homeroom teacher, as Nick took his seat. "First to arrive, as usual."

"Yes, ma'am, Miss Tulips," said Nick politely. "I thought I would take a few minutes to look over the composition I wrote for today."

"A fine idea," said Miss Tulips. "What title did you choose?"

" 'Self-Reliance,' " said Nick.

"Ah," said Miss Tulips. "Emerson's theme!"

"No, ma'am," said Nick, visibly blushing. "I wrote it myself."

"I only meant," said his teacher, "that it is an idea which we associate with the great American savant, Ralph Waldo Emerson."

"Shall I beat out the erasers for you, Miss Tulips?" volunteered Nick, who always made a point of being helpful about the classroom.

"How kind of you to offer, Nicholas," said Miss Tulips. "But I believe they have already been beaten this morning by Mr. Quincy."

"Another beating won't do them any harm," said Nick. Stepping up to the blackboard, he took the objects in question, and then excused himself from the room with a little bow, a quaint, courtly gesture which our hero had learned at the neighborhood cinema.

My young readers may be surprised to learn that Mr. Noxin's careful, religious principles did not prevent his sons' attending motion picture shows. But the groceryman

occasionally received free passes to the cinema, a gratuity
given to "Aunty" Noxin (as Nick's mother was known to
one and all) who once a week swept and mopped the local
theater as a further contribution to the family income,
and he was, moreover, insistent that his boys view only
moral and educational films, usually religious or historical in nature, such as Griffith's great *Birth of a Nation,*
which Nick had seen twice, inspiring him to master his
courtly bow.

Standing on the schoolhouse steps, Nick began to strike
the erasers together in a movement familiar I am sure
to all my young readers. Let us therefore leave him for
the moment, creating a thin white cloud visible to Mr.
Quincy from where he stood at the crossing, tending as
usual to the welfare of his young charges. Whether that
scrupulous gentleman took Nick's activities as a comment
on his own effectiveness regarding the beating of blackboard erasers I cannot say.

CHAPTER IV

Never
Say Die

☛

"A letter for you, Nick!"

Thus was our hero greeted by his youngest brother, Knox, as he returned home from school a week after the events recounted in the previous chapter. Knox was not yet of school age, and always met his returning brothers with some announcement, but seldom was it of such importance as the present tidings.

Nick took the envelope eagerly and devoured with his eyes the welcome name printed on it, which was his own, and the return address also, which was, as my young readers have suspected, the Editorial Offices of the Los Angeles *Times.* Having studied this information, Nick was importuned by his little brother to open the envelope and read what was inside, which he proceeded to do.

Our hero then placed the letter back in its envelope and with a thoughtful expression stood looking out of the window of his father's store, on which the legend

SYERECORG

was painted in neat if somewhat cracked and chipped letters.

"When do you start?" asked Knox.

"How much do they pay?" asked Obie.

"Did you get it, Nick?" asked Hardy, running breathlessly into the store. "Did you get it?"

"Yes, Hardy," said Nick, "I got it." Slowly he tore the letter into shreds and placed them into a trash can. "But I have decided not to take the job."

"Why not?" asked Obie. "Wouldn't they pay enough?"

"Newspapering," said Nick with a shrug, "is not for me. The Press, despite its boasting to the contrary, is in the grip of a privileged few who use the protection of the First Amendment to maintain a stranglehold on our nation's news. Not only do they thus weaken and corrupt the morality of our country, but they prevent honest men from attaining the platform from which they might be challenged."

"Gosh," said Hardy.

"Gee," said Knox.

"Who would have known it?" said Obie with a frown.

At this moment Mr. Noxin entered the store. "Bad news, son?" he asked, noticing the expression on Nick's face.

"The news is always *bad*," said our hero. "Why is it that these so-called *public* prints can only stress the negative side of American life, the crimes and the filth? Why is it that they can never treat the positive side, never list the accomplishments of those many honest men who labor in obscurity so as to lay the foundation stones of our national well-being? They, after all, are the majority."

"Well put," said his father. "I have myself noticed the generally gloomy tidings which the daily papers regularly herald with banner headlines. But what do we hear of the many good things done by the late, great President Harding? *Nothing!* All we read about is the Teapot Dome affair, to which he was only remotely connected, and only because of his generous and trusting nature."

"Frankly," said Nick, "I'm bored with the Teapot Dome affair. I think that America should get on with the ongoing business of making this nation great."

"As one who nearly became a successful and wealthy oilman," said Mr. Noxin, "I deeply resent the smears which the newspapers have dragged across the honest face of a noble profession, impugning the integrity of the great state of California by stressing the petty finaglings of a few corrupt individuals."

"Oil is the lifeblood of our nation," said Nick.

"Instead of being allowed to tend to the important business of state, our beloved President, Calvin Coolidge, is weighted down with a matter made burdensome only by the loud insistence of the public prints. Truly has it been said that the noisy wheel gets the grease."

"Thanks to the likes of the Los Angeles *Times*," said Nick.

"But if that is so," asked little Knox, "why don't you go to work for them and stick in some stories about the *good* side of oil?"

"That's a laugh," said Nick. "What can a lowly office boy do in a place where the power is held by a few hands? No, Knox, I shall adhere to my original intentions. The day will come when the newspapers will hear from me. They won't always be able to kick us Noxins around."

"It will be a great day for America," said Mr. Noxin proudly, "when the voice of the Little Man is heard in the corridors of power."

"I solemnly swear," said Nick, by chance laying his hand on the Montgomery Ward catalogue which lay next to the worn, dog-eared family Bible, in its place on the counter of the family store, where Mr. Noxin frequently consulted it during his theological disputations with his customers, "that whatever position of power and prestige is granted me when I grow up, I shall use it not only in the name of Justice, but for the true Freedom of the Press, which is not carping criticism of our basic institutions, but the triumphant heralding of the mighty accomplishments which have flourished under the enlightened sway of those selfsame institutions."

"But if you don't go to work for the newspaper," asked Hardy, "what will you do for a summer job?"

"Pick beans," declared Nick firmly, squaring his thin and only slightly humped shoulders. "Glad to be associated with a humble but honorable profession."

"Well said, Nick," said his father. "The hard fist of the man of the soil is a silent reproof of the limp fingers which hold the pen."

"Agriculture," said his son, "is the economic foundation of our great nation. It is as American as apple pie. Was not Thomas Jefferson our farmer President? Did not Abraham Lincoln follow the plow and split the rail? Yes, when the great call comes up yonder, this Noxin shall not be found wanting, but shall bring the simple, sturdy manners of the honest yeoman to the attention of the world!"

"Huzzah!" cried little Knox, tossing his cap in the air. "Let me pick beans, too!"

Our hero spent another sleepless night following his last day in school before vacation, but his thoughts were not agitated by the prospect of idle pleasures, time misspent in those pastimes to which so many boys of his age devote their summer vacations. No, Nick was excited over the humble prospect of picking beans, and in his mind's eye he saw his own fingers flying along the neat rows, turning a manly brown in the healthful heat of the California sun.

Doubtless, he thought, his industry would come to the attention of Squire Farley. Surely his employer would be able to distinguish the efforts of a native-born American from the lackadaisical habits of those dark-skinned people of the *sombrero*-shaded *siesta,* who, though perhaps well suited to labor requiring nimble hands and strong backs, were naturally unaspiring to higher, more responsible positions of authority. Soon enough, Nick thought, he would be singled out for such a position, perhaps as a timekeeper or a supervisor. Later, in all likelihood, he would rise to the management of one of the several Farley Farms, a field boss in his own right!

If this should happen, Nick planned to be an effective manager, who would rule his employees by the sheer force of his personality, not resorting to the blows with stick and fist so often used by people in similar capacities. For all their stupid, unaspiring ways, dark-skinned people did appreciate qualities of natural leadership. He would be like the plantation owners in *Birth of a Nation,* riding about the farm on a fine horse, receiving the respectful bows of his workers, responding with a smile and a manly salute from his riding crop. His success would not go unnoticed by Squire Farley, who could not help but make unfavorable comparisons between Nick and his worthless son. In time, the Squire would promote Nick to even greater responsibility, perhaps even taking him on as a partner at Farley Farms.

It was therefore with great hopes that Nick reported for work the next morning, leaving the house right after breakfast so as to put in a full day. After making several inquiries, he found Field Boss Snagg in the pump house, supervising repairs to a balky engine.

"Nick Noxin reporting for work, sir!" he announced briskly, giving Mr. Snagg a smart salute.

"You the kid with the gasket?" asked that individual with a scowl. "Hand it over."

"Gasket?" asked Nick. "No, sir, I'm here to pick beans."

"Well, why in blazes are you pestering *me?* Can't you see I'm busy?"

"The handbill said . . ." began Nick, holding out the announcement in question.

"Oh, *that* thing!" said the field boss with an unpleasant laugh as he used it to wipe the grease off his hands. "Must be two weeks old. Price is down to three cents a bushel. Wholesalers are putting the squeeze on us again. A pack of wily kikes. Buy cheap and sell dear, that's your Hebrew for you. So to make a decent profit we got to hire greasers at three cents a basket."

"But *I'm* not a greaser," said Nick, squaring his thin shoulders.

"So what?" said Snagg scornfully. "You want to do greaser work, you got to take greaser pay."

"I don't see how I can make much money at three cents a bushel," observed Nick.

"That's your lookout," said Snagg. "Take it or leave it."

"I have my pride," said Nick. "Besides, the handbill said ten cents a bushel, which I am told constitutes a *de facto* contract."

"You're beginning to sound like a troublemaker," said the field boss. "We don't like sea lawyers around here, kid. A lotta communists and anarchists these days, trying to get the greasers upset. You ain't a communist, are you?" Mr. Snagg produced a large monkey wrench.

"I should say not!" said Nick, offended at the suggestion.

"I'm glad to hear it," said Mr. Snagg. "Because Mr. Farley said if we find any communists hanging around here, to give 'em the *business*. Understand?" Leaning forward, the field boss put a thick, oily finger to our hero's chest, and shoved the wrench under his nose.

"Yes, sir," said Nick, stepping back. "Could you possibly make it five cents a bushel?"

"Not a chance," said Snagg. "We got a bunch of wetbacks coming in a day or so. Then we can knock it down to two cents a bushel, and maybe make a little money for a change."

"*Two* cents a bushel!" exclaimed Nick. "Why, that's hardly worth my while. . . ."

"To each his own," observed Mr. Snagg, returning to the pump house. "It's a free country."

As he left Farley Farms, feeling somewhat down in the mouth, Nick's mood was not improved by hearing the sound of an unpleasantly familiar voice: "Beans, beans, the musical fruit!"

Nick turned to find the taunting finger of Percy Squinch aimed at him. In the shade of one of the farm buildings, Frank Farley and his gang of toadies sat drinking pink lemonade and reading dime novels. Several corncob pipes were also in evidence.

"Well, well," said Frank. "It's Nick the Picker."

"Ha ha ha ha ha," laughed Percy. "That's a hot one, Frank!"

"Yes," observed Nick's tormentor, "it looks as though the grocersboy has graduated. Up to *field work*."

"I find nothing reprehensible in manual labor," said Nick. "The Bible tells us that we shall earn our bread by the sweat of our faces."

"Ugh!" cried Percy, with a mock expression of distaste. "What disgusting language."

"What do you expect when you associate with field workers?" said Frank. "They are little better than animals, my father tells me."

"Yes, Percy," said Nick, ignoring Frank. "I imagine you do find the mere mention of hard, honest work repugnant."

"Are you going to take that sitting down, Perce, old boy?" taunted Frank, who was always eager to start a fight so long as he was not himself involved.

"I . . . I certainly don't intend to engage in fisticuffs with a bean-picker," stammered Percy. "That would be beneath me."

"You would soon find," said Nick, "*who* would be beneath *whom*."

"I find this discussion tiresome," said Frank. "Come, fellows. Let us go up to the house and get some ginger snaps to go with our pink lemonade. Father would not like us to keep one of his field hands from work, besides."

"As it so happens," said Nick. "I am not working for your father."

"I have no interest whatsoever in your affairs," said Frank. "Come, fellows, and be sure to take all your things along with you. Some of these migrant laborers have very sticky fingers."

"Ha! Ha!" cried Percy with a clap of his hands. "Sticky Nick!"

"Sticky Nick the Picker," said Frank, sneering back at our hero as he led his band of toadies away.

"Gosh, Frank," said Archibald Pipple, "you sure have a great sense of humor."

"That reminds me," said Percy. "There's a nifty new Laurel & Hardy at the movies, Frank. Loads of laughs, they say. How about taking us to the matinee?"

"Oh," said Frank, putting his arm around his chief toady, "I think we can swing it, Perce."

Once again Nick and Frank Farley went their separate ways, our hero toward home, making a silent resolution that the Frank Farleys of the world would change their tune someday.

"Back so soon?" asked his father. "What happened, Nick?"

"The communists are upsetting the greasers, and the Jews have got the price of beans down so low that pickers get only three cents a bushel basket, and the only way Farley Farms can make a profit is to pay two cents a basket."

"Frankly," said Mr. Noxin, "I am not surprised. That is the strategy outlined in the Protocols of the Elders of Zion. The honest Christian worker will be caught between the communists and the Jews of Wall Street."

"Well," said Nick, "this is one honest Christian who won't be caught. Not at Farley Farms, at any rate. I told Boss Scragg that Noxins will not work for greaser wages."

"Good for thee, Nick," said his father. "But what *will* thee work for?"

"A decent day's pay," said Nick, sitting down on the store steps and taking out the cucumber and tomato sandwich his mother had packed for him in the waxed-paper wrapper from a loaf of bread. "Or a reasonable facsimile thereof."

"Spoken like a true Noxin!" said his father. "But, in the meantime, perhaps it is well that thee take on more responsibilities in the store."

CHAPTER V

Something
Comes
Nick's Way

☞

Thanks to Mr. Noxin, therefore, Nick did not remain idle following his discouraging experience at Farley Farms. He continued to work for his father, lugging in heavy crates of vegetables (for Mr. Noxin was plagued by a troublesome back) and making deliveries. In addition, he assisted in carrying out those many small economies which were the secret of the store's modest but steady profit. It was our hero's especial chore to inspect the piles of fresh fruit daily, picking out the rotted or bruised specimens. Likewise, he removed cracked and overaged eggs and moldy or vermin-infested flour from the bins. These he carried into the kitchen, for his mother possessed the culinary skills necessary to transform these damaged comestibles into delicious pies, the sale of which represented a considerable portion of the Noxin income.

Because of his superior mathematical ability, Nick was also given the responsibility of keeping his father's books, an assignment complicated by several refinements introduced into the usual double-entry system by Mr. Noxin, who, as my young readers are by now fully aware, was fond of improvements of all kinds, a typical characteristic of the Western spirit.

"Pies, as such," he explained to Nick, "are not groceries, as such. We shall keep the pie account here." Lifting up what appeared to be the bottom of his cash drawer, Mr. Noxin took out a small black book on which was written the three letters "P.I.E."

"Pie," read Nick aloud.

"Profits," explained Mr. Noxin, "In Excess. As thee knows, we keep regular accounts here, in the ledger." Opening this large volume, placed next to the Bible on the counter, the groceryman explained to his boy the method by which loss was subtracted from gain, the figure at the bottom signifying the true profit, or "net."

"I see," said Nick, his alert eye scanning the neat columns, "that you list on the loss side all spoiled produce. Would that include the fruit, eggs, and flour with which Mother makes her pies?"

"Of course. Anything less would be less than the truth," said Mr. Noxin. "I have always called a spade a spade, have I not? Rotten food is rotten food, and I hope that thee never sees the day when N. O. Noxin calls rotten food *fresh!* As I told thee, Nick, pies are pies, groceries are groceries. What happens to the spoiled

produce is no one's business but our own. Some feed it
to pigs, which they butcher and sell. Others throw it
away, a sinful waste. We make pies from it. As groceries,
of course, it is a total loss."

"Of course," said Nick, examining the P.I.E. accounts.
"But I see here that you deduct its cost from the pie
profits."

"What would thee have me do?" asked his father. "We
paid for it, did we not? As groceries it may be a loss, but
as pie makings it is an expense. So with the sawdust on
our floor, a loss as lumber, but sold as floor cleaner. Everything in business, Nick, is relative."

Despite the demands on his time of these many chores,
Nick did not lose sight of his future goals. It was his habit
to rise before the rest of the family, indeed at the crack
of dawn. Our hero would then hike two miles from Poco
Lobo to Bragadura Cove, an indentation of the California coastline favored by picnickers and other seekers
of diversion and pleasure. At his chosen hour, the cove
was usually deserted, and Nick would devote himself to
improving his oratorical powers. Following Mr. Cosmo
Castle's instructions, our hero would station himself at
the water's edge, two rocks held in his hands and one
pressed between his knees. He would place a flat stone
on his head, and having previously filled his mouth with
wet, salty pebbles picked up at the ocean's edge, Nick
would recite passages of oratory earlier committed to
memory, accompanying the words with suitable gestures.

"I have noticed," Nick remarked to Professor Castle
one day, "that the weight and substance of the pebbles

have produced a noticeable sag to the pouches of my cheeks. Will not this deformity perhaps act to neutralize the improvement in my style of delivery?"

"Not at all," he was assured by the dignified master of the forensic art. "You will find in later life that highly developed jowls are an invaluable asset when assuming a posture requiring expressions of indignation and outrage. Let me show you what I mean."

Drawing himself up to his full height of five feet, two inches, the professor caused his blue eyes to flash in marked contrast to his rubicund complexion: "OUT-RRRRAGGEOUS!" he boomed. "UNHEARRRD OF EFFRRRRRRRONTERRRRY! AN INSULT TO THE GRRRREAT AMERRRRRICAN PUBLIC!" By way of emphasis he vibrated his heavy jowls in magisterial fashion, somewhat dampening the immediate area with a sublime spray.

Relaxing and lowering his voice to conversational tones, Professor Castle went on to explain to his star pupil that a certain fullness of jowl connotes respectability. "We recall that the traitor Cassius had a 'lean and hungry look,'" he pointed out. "Fleshiness something less than grossness is to be desired. You will also find, Noxin, that a full jowl is especially conducive to effective expressions of self-righteousness. I speak not of wrathful denunciations, but rather of earnest statements of high moral purpose, delivered as if one's cheeks were half-filled with mashed potatoes and gravy."

So it was that Nick went daily to Bragadura Cove and practiced his oratory in the manner I have already de-

scribed. On one such morning, a week or so after his
decision regarding agricultural endeavors, our hero noticed that a small vessel was riding at anchor in the cove
when he arrived. As he stood declaiming and waving his
arms about, he saw a boat leave the vessel and head for
shore.

Not wishing to appear inquisitive, yet reluctant to
surrender his favorite spot, our hero stood his ground
and continued to address the rolling surf as the boat
put ashore nearby. Though he avoided staring at the
strangers, Nick could not but note that the boat was
packed with specimens of that branch of humanity com-
monly known as "Celestials," though referred to by his
father (employing the common parlance of the day) as
"Chinamen."

No sooner had the boat grounded than the sound of a
motor vehicle was heard, and a truck of the sort used to
convey livestock appeared on the beach. The Celestials
were escorted rather rudely into the truck, chattering
shrilly in the manner of their tribe. After a canvas had
been dropped over the back of the conveyance com-
pletely concealing them from view, the truck drove off.

During the passage of these events, which took less
time than it takes to describe them, Nick stood reciting
to the waves. One of the landing party approached him
cautiously, head held to one side, as if witnessing an
occurrence beyond his comprehension. Thrusting his face
close to our hero's, he regarded Nick with one curious
eye, the other held shut in a tight squint, suggesting
skepticism, even distrust. The man's features were nar-

row and sharp, a pointedness set off by a closely clipped
moustache and shadowed by a snap-brim Panama hat
with a red-white-and-blue striped band.

"Hey, kid," he said in a gruff whisper. "You okay?"

"Ob cose Ah'b ohay!" said Nick indignantly, his heavy
jowls shaking. "An' don' caw may *keh!*"

"What? What did you say?" The squint-eyed man (for
it now appeared to be a permanent disfigurement, the re-
sult of a scar that marred his eyebrow and upper cheek)
cupped one ear. "Speak up!"

"DON' CAW MAY *KEH!*"

"What's that you're saying, kid? You have a cleft palate
or something?"

In desperation, Nick spat out his pebbles. "I said,
'Don't call me *kid!*' My name is Nicholas Noxin, and I
am perfectly all right. I happen to be practicing oratory,
as is my daily custom."

"No kidding?" asked the squint-eyed man, a question
that did not seem to demand an answer, and Nick did
not provide one. "What did you say your name was?"

"Nick Noxin," replied our hero, wondering what possible interest his identity held for the sharp-featured
stranger.

"Listen, Nick, how would you like to earn some money?" The stranger smiled as he said this, and Nick noticed in his quick way that the smile was flecked with
gold.

"So long as it's honestly come by," said our hero,
squaring his thin shoulders. The flat stone on his head
took this opportunity to depart.

"Come, Nick," said the squint-eyed man. "Do I look like the kind of guy who would propose something *not* honest?"

"Appearances," said Nick, "are often deceptive."

"How right you are," said the stranger. "Like for example what you saw here this morning. Now, to a suspicious type, it might look like . . . why, like an illegal importation of Chinese immigrants!"

"I know nothing of such matters," said Nick.

"Good for you," said the squint-eyed man, taking out a money clip and extracting a five-dollar bill. "And you be sure to keep it that way." Reaching out, he tucked the money into Nick's coat pocket.

"Oh, sir!" said Nick, removing the bill and putting it in his snap-lock purse. "That was not necessary. I was merely doing what any self-respecting citizen should do, acquainting myself with nothing that does not pertain to my own affairs."

"That," said the squint-eyed man, "is just what I want to hire you to do. In the future, Nick, when you see the *Shady Lady* riding out there in the cove, I want you to keep right on minding your own business. And if you should happen to see any uniforms around when you arrive, or happen to spot automobiles with 'P.D.' painted on them, I will make it worth your while to go someplace else and make speeches. How does that sound?" he asked, placing another five-dollar bill in Nick's pocket.

"I believe I could oblige," said Nick, with a nod.

"You see, Nick, I am a businessman who likes privacy, and that is why I have picked this lonely spot and early hour to conduct my affairs. But there are some people, mostly nosy citizens and public officials, whose small minds might jump to conclusions based on my eccentric habits. So your cooperation, Nick, will be well rewarded."

"I shall be glad to assist you to the best of my ability, Mr. . . . uh . . . *sir*."

"My name is B. Franklin Alibi," said the squint-eyed gentleman. "I am of Mediterranean extraction, but my parents named me after the American whose portrait appears on the penny postcard, as a token of their loyalty to their new home."

Mr. Alibi having extended his hand, Nick took it in his own, and in the exchange of friendship and trust which followed, he accidentally dropped the stone held between his knees on Mr. Alibi's well-shined, two-tone shoe.

"Ai!" cried that gentleman, in his pain involuntarily giving our hero a box on the ear.

"Ow!" cried Nick, in a consequent spasm inadvertently kicking sand in the face of Mr. Alibi, who, in his struggles to splash water in his eyes, accidentally knocked Nick into the ocean, where he was seized by an outgoing wave, and would surely have drowned had it not been for the vigilance of the sailors by the boat, who rushed in and pulled our hero out, thus saving him from an untimely fate.

Unfortunately, the sailors had misunderstood the sequence of events they had just witnessed, and fell on Nick with fists, feet, and pistol butts (with which they were plentifully provided), and would have rendered him senseless had not Mr. Alibi eventually rescued our hero. Even so, Nick departed from the cove bearing a number of painful contusions, along with the two five-dollar bills, which (it must be said) provided ample compensation for the injuries sustained.

As he neared home, Nick brushed the sand from his clothing and quickened his step. Because of his conversation with Mr. Alibi, he was late for breakfast, and hastened therefore to join his father in the kitchen, the rest of the family having already departed.

"What happened to *thee?*" asked his father, who was so startled by his son's appearance that he removed the splinter from his mouth with which he was practicing the praiseworthy habit of dental hygiene by removing bits of breakfast steak lodged between his teeth.

"I was hit," said Nick, helping himself to a bowl of water gruel from the pot simmering on the stove, "by a livestock truck."

"Did thee get the license number?" asked his father. "We'll sue!"

"No," said Nick, pulling one of the bills out of his pocket. "But the man gave me this."

"Better than nothing," said Mr. Noxin, reaching forward and taking it. "But next time, Nick, be sure to get the number, besides. Opportunity knocks, but we must open the door."

"I could not agree more, Father," said Nick, attending to his hearty breakfast with a relish that boded well for his quick recovery.

CHAPTER VI

Nick Finds
a New Patron

☞

Over the succeeding weeks, Mr. B. Franklin Alibi made several irregular visits to Bragadura Cove, and Nick furthered his acquaintance with that benevolent gentleman, always to his personal profit. During these meetings, our hero often enough had opportunities to contemplate the adage which he had earlier recited to Mr. Alibi concerning the deceptiveness of appearances. One day a boatload of what appeared to be our little brown brothers from the Philippine Islands were rowed ashore to be ushered without ceremony into the waiting livestock truck, and at a later date, out of that same truck was herded a crowd of young women whose flour-sacking dresses suggested rural origins, and who, not without protestation and cries of pain and fear, were escorted with whips and cattle prods aboard the waiting boat from the *Shady Lady*.

Nor was Mr. Alibi engaged in ferrying passengers only. One morning a boatload of crates labeled "XXXX WHISKEY: Product of Great Britain" was conveyed ashore, and on another occasion, boxes marked "BROWNING AUTO. RIFLES: 1 DOZ." were lugged by sweating sailors into a sleek black Cadillac hearse that appeared on the beach to receive them. Large cartons of pharmaceutical supplies were also conveyed past our hero, marked "MORPHINE," LAUDANUM," and "COCAINE," all of which would have given a less trusting lad cause for suspicion.

"Did I not know better, sir," said Nick to Mr. Alibi with a chuckle as he took a ten-dollar bill from his patron, "I should think that you were engaged in some kind of smuggling operation."

"So you might," chuckled Mr. Alibi in return. "But I spotted you immediately for a smarter kid than that. It takes real brains to see through false appearances, like the strange hour of the day, the loneliness of this spot, and the unusual cargoes coming in. That is why I consider you such a valuable member of my suspicious-looking operation, Nick." With a wink, Mr. Alibi stuffed an extra five-dollar bill into our hero's pocket.

Many another boy would have made an ostentatious display of his sudden wealth, but Nick was not the sort to parade himself before his family and friends, nor did he seek to rival Frank Farley in the noisily public consumption of phosphates. Instead, he kept his money safely

hidden in a number of places, and continued to work
daily in his father's store.

Nick made his deliveries every afternoon, using for
that purpose a cart ingeniously fashioned by Mr. Noxin
from an old baby carriage which, though missing one
wheel, was quite adequate for the purpose. On one such
occasion, Nick was making his way home late in the day
when he was startled by the sound of an automobile horn
behind him (at the time of this story a rare occurrence
indeed in Poco Lobo), and was even more surprised to
find Banker Aeneas Briggs waving to him from the open
window of his gleaming Studebaker limousine.

"Come here, boy!" cried the Croesus of Poco Lobo.

"I?" asked Nick, looking around, but not forgetting
in his confusion to observe correct grammatical usage.

"Yes, *you!* Nicholas Noxin! That is your name, isn't
it?"

"Yes, sir, it is, Mr. Briggs, sir," said our hero, recovering himself quickly and approaching the Studebaker.
"Can I deliver something for you?"

"Indeed you can!" crowed the banker. "Deliver yourself, one Nicholas Noxin, right into this seat next to me,
and be quick about it. Climb in, my boy! Climb in!"

Nick could not but note that the banker's smiling face
was a marked contrast to his usual dour manner, which
only increased our hero's astonishment at the unexpected
invitation.

"But . . ." he stammered. "My . . . my delivery
cart . . ."

"Leave it where it is, my boy. It will be there when

you return. I have a proposition to put to you which will be very much to your advantage. Climb in!"

"Well," said Nick, reluctantly. "I'm due home in a few minutes."

"Wonderful!" crowed the banker joyfully, throwing open the car door. "I like that in a boy! Family duty before pleasure! Well, Nicholas, let old Aeneas Briggs provide the means. Climb in! Climb in! What I have to say can be said between here and your father's humble place of business. Free and clear, however, if I recall aright. Free and clear."

With a quickening beat of his heart, Nick let go of the handle of his delivery cart, which slowly overturned as he climbed into the back seat of the luxurious vehicle.

"Now!" said the richest man in Poco Lobo, having given directions to his liveried Negro chauffeur and settled back in his corner with a smile. "If I could grant you one wish, Nicholas Noxin, what would it be? Hmm?"

"Why," said our hero, "being a normal American boy, I should like very much to rise in this world."

"*Ah!* I knew it! I knew it!" cried the banker. "A fine boy, a bright boy, a superb boy! An *American* boy! And rise you shall, Nicholas Noxin, and rise you shall!" he crowed, rubbing his hands until Nick could hear the skin squeak. "You are aware, are you not," continued Mr. Briggs, "that I have the means at my disposal to enable you to vastly improve your present station in life, which, though honorable, is admittedly humble?"

"Money helps, they say," said Nick.

"Money helps!" cried the banker. "Oh, ha ha ha! *Wit!*
I like that in a boy, indeed I do! Money helps! I should
say it does! Money . . . why, money is the bread of life!
I mean . . . the staff of bread. . . . Drat, how does that
go?"

"Bread," said Nick, "is the staff of life."

"Don't you believe it," said the banker, "for one minute! How does one get one's bread . . . ?"

"With the sweat of his face," said Nick.

"Yes, of course," said the banker, "indeed one does.
But he gets *paid* for that sweat, does he not? With good
old *money?* Unless, of course, he lives in slavery, as in
communist Russia. No money, no bread. That's the democratic rule, is it not? After all, what is it makes the world
go round?"

"Planetary motion?"

"Is that what they teach in school these days? No, my
boy, it's MONEY! Money! Money! Money!

"Well," said Nick, "we Noxins certainly could use
some."

"Ah! *Frankness!* I like that in a boy, also. Yes indeed
I do! From your earliest days, Nick, I have had my eye
on you. There, Aeneas, I have said—a thousand times if
I said it once—there goes the most *likely* boy in town.
Dutiful, reasonable, and *frank.*"

"Thank you, sir," said Nick, blushing visibly. "I try
to do my best to obey the teachings of the Friends."

"Ah, an excellent faith!" crowed Banker Briggs, just
then looking out the window as the Studebaker passed

the solid brick front of the largest building in Poco Lobo, his bank. "Regular depositors, regular as rain! Though I, myself, happen to be of the Episcopal persuasion, which, alas! has no temple within convenient range of town. Except in Las Plugas, where the priest has low-church leanings. . . . Where was I?"

"You were talking about money," said Nick.

"Ah, yes! Now I remember! I'm about to make you a very handsome proposition, considering your lowly station in life. Yes, indeed! How does that sound?"

"Fine," said our hero with a smile. "So far."

"Ah!" cried the banker with another clap of his hands. "I like a *hard nose* in a boy best of all! A long nose is a sign of *character,* and a *hard* nose guarantees persistence. You have the makings of a very long nose, if I'm not mistaken," said the banker, regarding our hero's profile with an appraising squint (like most successful businessmen, Mr. Briggs considered himself a perceptive judge of budding physiognomy) "and I'll do my best to harden it."

"Sir?" asked Nick, who was somewhat put off by the banker's allusion to his nose, which inadvertently brought the unpleasant fable by Collodi to mind, so much so that our hero grabbed for his ears.

"I intend," announced the banker slowly, punctuating each word by stabbing the air with his finger, "to hire you for the remainder of the summer, as a special assistant to me, in the Tri-Mutual Guaranteed Trust and Loan Company of Poco Lobo. And at a handsome salary, also. What would you say to ten dollars a week?"

"Oh, thank you, sir!" cried our hero."Oh, thank you so very much, Mr. Briggs!"

"I like that in a boy," said the banker. "Gratitude. Can't be beat as a sign of character. Now," he said, "as to details. You are aware, are you not, of the existence of Large 'S' Enterprises, Ltd., a subsidiary of the Tri-Mutual Guaranteed Trust and Loan Company?"

"No," said Nick, blushing visibly. "I'm afraid I am not, sir."

"Ah, honesty!" said Mr. Briggs. "The prime virtue of them all! Well, Nicholas, Large 'S' Enterprises is many things to many people, but so far as you are concerned, it is a Charity Bazaar in Long Beach, California. Among your other duties, your chief responsibility will be to serve, once a week, as bag (ahem) as *bank* messenger. Besides that, you will work as my confidential assistant, and have an opportunity to learn the banking business in general, et cetera, et cetera. Your confidential duties I shall explain to you when you start work, this Monday, seven A.M. *sharp*. As for the rest, you will find it spelled out in this envelope, along with ten dollars, which you will use to buy yourself a decent suit of clothes . . ."

"Oh, thank you, sir!"

". . . and which is your first week's salary. You are quite welcome. PULL UP TO THE PUMP, YOU STUPID NIGGER!" cried the banker suddenly, leaning forward to rap on the glass partition, the Studebaker (I neglected to mention) having come to a stop by the curb in front of Mr. Noxin's store.

"Yassuh, boss," came the feeble response from behind

the glass, as the chauffeur hastened in his lethargic way
to do Mr. Briggs's bidding.

"Slower than molasses in January," grumbled the
banker.

Nick felt a hot blush suffuse his face. —Someday, he
thought to himself —I, too, will have a Studebaker and
a nigger driver.

"Fill her up, Mr. Briggs, sir?" asked Mr. Noxin, bend-
ing down to the half-opened window and pulling the sole
remaining forelock on his otherwise bald head. "NICK!"
he cried, seeing his son seated next to the most powerful
man in Poco Lobo. Dropping the hose nozzle, Mr. Noxin
snatched open the door. "What are you doing here?
What have you done?"

"Your boy has kindly consented to accept a business
proposition which I have put to him, Noxin," said Banker
Briggs, leaning forward with a smile. "A likely young
man, Noxin. I like him."

"Why . . . thank you . . . thank you very much, Mr.
Briggs, sir," stammered Mr. Noxin.

"Out you go, my boy. Don't forget, seven A.M. . . .
sharp!"

"Well, Nick," said his father. "You heard what Mr.
Briggs said. Hop out of there and be quick about it!"

"A fine boy," said the banker as our hero hastened to
obey his employer and his father. "If he works hard and
keeps his mouth shut and his nose to the grindstone, he'll
rise far in this world."

"Thank you, sir," said Mr. Noxin, closing the door and

wiping his fingerprints off with a rag. "My . . . my regards to Mrs. Briggs," he added, as the limousine sped off
in a cloud of dust.

"I'm sorry, Father," said Nick, as he placed the hose
back on its hook, "but I shall have to go back for my
delivery cart."

"Forget the cart—for the moment, son," said his father.
"What sort of business proposition did Mr. Briggs make
thee?"

"I'm to go to work as his special assistant," said Nick.
"Something to do with charity . . ."

"Charity!" cried Mr. Noxin. "I do hope it has not come
to that, Nick! May it never be said that a son of N. O.
Noxin was a recipient of charity! Better that thy mother
scrub floors on her bended knee . . . !"

"No, no," said Nick. "Dispensing charity, not receiving
it. I believe this letter explains everything."

"That is different," said Mr. Noxin, taking the letter
and opening it. "Does not the Scripture place charity
above faith and hope, and teach us that it is better to give
than receive?"

"I shall receive *something*," said Nick. "Mr. Briggs has
offered me a salary of ten dollars a week for the rest of
the summer."

"I shall open a savings account for thee in my name,"
said his father, putting on his eyeglasses and sitting down
on the store steps with Mr. Briggs's letter, the ten dollars
placed safely in his shirt pocket. "Let us see, now, what
the nature of this charity work is. I do hope some effort

is made to distinguish worthy as opposed to fraudulent objects of philanthropy."

The letter soon put Mr. Noxin's fears to rest. The good work carried out by Mr. Briggs's organization involved arrangements by which illegally entered immigrants could be gainfully employed while awaiting deportation, a certain percentage of their earnings set aside to defray train fare, and other costs, the rest to be used to cover the expenses of board, room, and keep during the afore-said period—which period, particularly during the grow-ing and harvesting season, could amount to several months—and if any balance should accrue, such monies would be returned to the General Fund, on deposit in Mr. Briggs's bank and audited regularly by the trustees of the Fund.

Since the vagaries of apprehending illegal immigrants were such as to gainsay a guarantee of regular income to the General Fund, the charitable organization sponsored a number of bazaars throughout the Western states. These harmless affairs, by raffling off wholesome hams raised on the farms which employed the detained immigrants, were the chief source of operating assets handled by the chari-table organization. Nick's chief responsibility, while learning the banking and charity business, was to make weekly trips to one such bazaar in Long Beach, where he would exchange an empty suitcase for a filled one.

"Well," said Mr. Noxin, mollified by what he had read and, according to the final instructions, setting fire to the letter with a stove match he happened to be holding in his mouth, "it seems to be a worthwhile endeavor, indeed, enabling the recipients of charity to maintain their pride and self-esteem by *earning* the benefits bestowed."

"And I shall be *learning* the bank business, besides!"

"A grand opportunity, son," said Mr. Noxin. "I have always ranked Mr. Briggs as a foremost citizen of this town, county, and state," he went on, "even though he is an Episcopalian and a member of the Rotary, instead of a Friend and a Mason. But never did I dream that he would take an active interest in the future of a member of my family. Still, he is childless, and perhaps wishes to earn through the power of his influence what he cannot otherwise obtain, the gratitude of a worthy youth."

"Is it indeed so unusual," asked Nick, "for a man of wealth to take interest in the future of a likely lad? I speak, of course, in general not particular terms, you understand."

"I understand that it is indeed not unusual in this great land of opportunity for an older capitalist to take a younger man, talented but impoverished, under his wing. But never before in my experience has it happened."

"Then," said Nick, "this is a truly historical occasion!"

"It certainly is a first," said Mr. Noxin, "in the annals of Poco Lobo. . . ."

"First in Poco Lobo," said Nick, "then . . . the World!"

"Thy ambition is praiseworthy," said his father, "and a man's reach must exceed his grasp, or what are fingers for? But do try to remember, Nick, that all Mr. Briggs has promised thee is summertime employment in his bank, and not the presidency. . . ."

"I realize that," said Nick with a modest smile. "But it would not be the first time that a poor but talented boy was able to mount to the highest office this nation can provide!"

"I was speaking," said his father, "of the presidency of Mr. Briggs's bank. But, no mind. It is certainly my feeling, Nick, that Mr. Briggs is testing thee, to see if thee is qualified for greater responsibilities. Perhaps a clerkship, as a start, where thee can continue to master the intricacies of double-entry accounting, someday to qualify as a Certified Public Accountant, no negligible position in this land of capitalized free enterprise. No matter how thee looks at it, Nick, it certainly is a grand opportunity. I hope thee takes full advantage of it."

"I can't wait to tell Mother, Obie, Hardy, and Knox!"

"Yes," said his father, pulling out his railroad watch. "This calls for a celebration, Nick. We'll close the store early tonight."

True to his word, Mr. Noxin pulled down the shade on the front door to his commercial establishment (on which was cleverly painted the message: "SORRY TO HAVE MISSED YOUR BUSINESS, N. O. NOXIN, PROP.") ten minutes before the regular closing time that evening, something which he had not done since the armistice had been declared at the end of the Great War.

CHAPTER VII

Nick's
Interest
Is Compounded

My young reader must not think that our hero's new-found opportunity blinded him to his earlier good fortune. In the days which followed his thrilling interview with Aeneas Briggs, busy as they were with errands and filled with plans and expectations, Nick continued to report at the crack of dawn to Bragadura Cove, there to practice his oratory and wait for Mr. Alibi. By rising a half hour earlier, and running to the beach and back, Nick calculated that he could continue to meet his prior obligation while taking on the added responsibilities, although his breakfast time was cut to five minutes. A bicycle, of course, would have been of immeasurable assistance, and Nick resolved to put aside a portion of his

bank salary weekly for that purpose, a resolve which his
father approved, not only because it would provide opportunity for healthful exercise while enabling his son to
continue his oratorial practice, but because it promoted,
by saving money for a practical end, good mercantile
habits:

"He who floats on credit, soon gets drowned in debit,"
was one of Mr. Noxin's favorite mottos. "Besides," he
added, "thy birthday is coming soon, Nick, and thee deserves something special."

Thus the remainder of the week sped quickly by, and
we next encounter our hero on the most important Monday morning of his young life, making a few final touches
to his appearance, carefully brushing his unruly curls so
as to part them in the precise middle of his skull, that
being the neat fashion of the day, the process facilitated
by an application of the contents of his mother's lard jar,
as well as with brisk strokes with matching scrub-brushes,
also furnished by Aunty Noxin. For a mirror, Nick used
the bottom half of the bathroom window, which had
been painted on the outside to guarantee privacy while
the top half provided light, the whole arrangement a
demonstration of economy, utility, and ingenuity, to
which Mr. Noxin was fond of calling visitors' attention.

Besides his neatly dressed hair, Nick had in other ways
undergone a magical transformation from the sun-tanned,
overalled and barefooted boy we first encountered, thanks
to the attentions of the local clothier, Abraham A. Israel,
who had outfitted his young customer in what that redoubtable individual declared was "jiffy time."

Nick was dressed in a dapper simulated "Palm Beach" suit, "just the thing for summertime wear," an Arrow shirt with a stiff "Warren G. Harding" collar ("on sale this month") and a tasteful necktie of black near-silk with white polka dots. On his feet were new Buster Brown shoes, two toned with pointed toes, the recently introduced Young Mister model, very much the thing that year, according to Mr. Israel, who happened to find his last pair on a high shelf in the storeroom. They were rather a tight fit, but Mr. Israel made them more comfortable by adjusting the price. Certainly the yellow-and-black shoes were just the ticket to set off the light tan of his vested suit and the black-and-red band around the boater which the clothier threw in to honor the occasion of a new customer, the sweatband having been somewhat stained by the dissatisfied brow of an older one.

As he stood on the front porch, ready to depart for his first day of salaried employment, Nick looked very much like a freshly turned out young man of the world, and Aunty Noxin, understandably moved by the transformation, departed for the kitchen with her apron raised to her eyes.

"Aw, Ma," said Obie, perhaps a bit jealous because of the figure his younger brother cut, "He's just goin' down to the *bank*."

"Well, Nick," said his father, for the first time in our hero's life taking his hand and shaking it in a man-to-man grip, "have a good day at the office."

"Thank you, Father," said Nick. "I'll be home for lunch."

"So long, Nick," said Hardy. "Don't take any wooden *nick*els!"

"Heh heh heh heh," laughed our hero. "I'll try *hard* not to!"

"G'bye, Nick," said little Knox. "Here's a penholder I made from a peanut-butter jar."

"Why, thank you, Knoxie," said Nick, taking the article in question, the original purpose of which had been obscured with applications of colored paper and paste. "I'm sure I'll put it to good use."

"There's something inside it, already," said Knox, eagerly.

Reaching in, Nick took out a cardboard box, rather heavy for its size. On the cover in fancy gilt letters were the words "F. Schwartzgelt & Son: Jewelers."

"Open it! Open it!" cried Knox, barely able to conceal his excitement.

With trembling fingers, Nick did as he was bid, and discovered in its nest of white cotton a gleaming new WATCH!

"Gosh," he said, reading the lettering on the dial through blurred eyes, "a W-Waterbury watch."

"And it runs, too!" said Knox. "Wind it, Nick! Wind it!"

"It's already wound," said Hardy.

"The cost will have to come out of your next paycheck, Nick," said his father. "The clothes ate up every last bit of Mr. Briggs's ten dollars. But I knew you'd want one. You'll find that it will be the smartest dollar you ever spent."

"What time *is* it, Nick?" asked Knox.

"Gosh," said Nick. "Six-forty-five! I'd better be on my way!"

Wiping at his eyes with his stiff new handkerchief, Nick turned and strode manfully away, the new watch already placed in the pocket of his vest. When he arrived at the bank he consulted it once again and found that the trip took him exactly seven and three-quarters minutes. He was early, therefore, and the door to the bank was locked.

Exactly seven and a quarter minutes later, Mr. Aeneas Briggs's Studebaker stopped in front of the bank and the chauffeur hopped out and opened the rear door.

"Well, well," said Banker Briggs as he clambered out of his seat. "Early, I see." Knocking the chauffeur's hand off his arm with an impatient gesture, the Croesus of Poco Lobo squinted at the peanut-butter jar in the hands of his newest employee. "What's that?"

"A penholder, sir," said Nick.

"Well," said Mr. Briggs, "you can put horehounds in it for all I care. You won't have any use for *pens* in this job. The day I catch you *writing* is the day you collect your last pay from *me*."

Without further ado, the banker brushed past the puzzled Nick and, taking a large ring of heavy-looking keys from his pocket, he selected one and opened the bank door. "Another thing," added the banker, taking our hero's arm and ushering him inside, "when I say 'Seven sharp' I don't mean *early*, I mean *on the button*. Gives the place a bad name to have loiterers hanging around the front door. Next thing you know, people will be asking *questions*. Is that understood?"

"Oh, yes, sir," said Nick. "I won't do it again."

"See that you don't," said the crusty banker, as he led Nick past the silent and empty tellers' cages toward his office at the rear of the building. "I have problems enough without *questions*."

Taking out his key ring once again, Mr. Briggs unlocked his office door. "Well, here we are," he said, preceding his employee into the room. "My home away from home."

The banker's office, though large and high-ceilinged, was simply and functionally furnished with an oaken, rolltop desk and a springback chair, under the casters of which a ragged bit of rug had been placed so as to protect the oiled floorboards, which gave the room a faint odor of kerosene. Along one wall were several wooden file cabinets above which was a picture of the American flag and the motto, "In God We Trust."

Placed next to the desk was a bent-wood chair with a plywood seat, to which Mr. Briggs motioned Nick as he sat down behind his desk, unlocked it, and slid it open. Inside, Nick could not but note, was a telephone, a tray of pens and pencils, and a calendar pad.

"Well," said Banker Briggs, tearing Sunday from the calendar (at that time, I should explain to my young readers, even banks kept a six-day week), "another day, another dollar." He chuckled and turned to Nick. "The great thing about money, my boy, is that it isn't *union-*

ized. Keeps working for you day and night, Sundays and holidays, too. Working, working, working. Bet you never looked at money that way, hey, boy?"

"No, sir, I never have," said Nick.

"Well, you will. You will. Nothing like proximity to get you thinking about a thing. Nossireebob! Whenever I want real money thoughts, I come down here after everybody's gone, unlock the vault, and *roll in the stuff!* Hee, hee, hee, hee!"

"Heh, heh, heh, heh," laughed Nick.

"That's just between you, me, and the gatepost, you understand," said the banker, poking Nick in the chest with a forefinger, made hard by a small rubber cap, something like a thimble, which persons accustomed to counting large sums of paper money often wear. "Like everything that goes on here, understand?"

"Oh, I shan't say a word, sir!" cried Nick.

"Nobody'd believe you, anyway," said the banker. "My word against yours. *You* didn't believe me, did you?"

"Why, no! No, sir, I didn't as a matter of fact."

"You *didn't?* Thought I was *lying,* did you?"

"Oh, *no!* I . . . I thought . . . Well, to be perfectly honest, sir, I thought you were joking."

"I *like* that," said Banker Briggs. " 'To Be Perfectly Honest. . . .' Those are my sentiments exactly. I'd like them on my tombstone someday. . . ." The banker looked dreamily out his window at the clapboards and peeling paint of the building across the alleyway.

"Oh, heaven forbid, sir!" cried our hero.

"Hey? What was that?"

". . . That you'd ever *have* a tombstone, I meant, sir."

"Yes, it's too bad, isn't it? Well, I've got my best years ahead of me. Which reminds me, boy, time's a-wasting."

Rising, the banker took out his ring of keys once again and opened a small closet door which Nick had not seen before, half-hidden as it was behind one of the file cabinets. Inside the closet was a chair like the one beside the desk.

"Here you are," said Mr. Briggs. "An office all to yourself."

"But there's no light," said Nick.

"Light? There'll be sufficient light for your purposes, my boy. But I want you to use your *ears*, especially."

"My ears?"

"Yes, *these* things," said the banker, emphasizing his point by twisting one of the appendages in question.

"Ow! Ouch!" cried Nick, the appendage being his own.

"I'm not paying you to ask stupid questions," said the banker. "Now get in there and listen sharp."

"I thought I was going to learn the bank business," said Nick.

"Believe me, you will," said the banker, speeding him into the closet with his foot. "Get a hustle on, now, before my people start arriving. Sit down, keep quiet . . . and *listen*."

Sitting down on the rather small and uncomfortable chair, Nick looked up at his employer. "What shall I listen *for?*" he asked.

"Let me explain," said Mr. Briggs. "You see, my boy, I am a man beset by many enemies. I am rich, and may seem therefore powerful to such as yourself, but I can assure you that the more rich you become, the weaker you are, because open to vicious attack from petty, envious people, even those in your own generous employ!"

"I hope to find that out myself someday," said Nick, modestly.

"You will find it out right here and now," said the banker, "and at no cost to yourself, indeed to your profit. When I shut this door, you will notice two pinpricks of light, to your left and to your right. The left-hand pinprick is the gentlemen's washroom, the right-hand pinprick is (ahem) the ladies'. I want you to pay particular attention to what goes on in each of those facilities, my boy, and to keep a sharp ear for evidence of . . . betrayal."

"Betrayal? Of what?"

"Of *whom,* you numbskull! Of *me,* the Tri-Mutual Guaranteed Trust and Loan. Of the *country,* our great wonderful democratic nation of free enterprise. It's all the same thing. Remember the words of our beloved president, 'The Business of America Is Business.' And what is the business of *business?* Banking. And what is the business of banking? Security. Too many leaks empty the pail. Do I make myself clear?"

"Perfectly," said Nick, who was hardly the numbskull his employer made him out to be. "A sieve gathers no sand."

"Security," said the banker. "That's what banking is

all about. What are vaults for? Locks? Bars? Bolts? Why, if money were for the taking, who would stand in line to receive it?" He shook his head grimly. "Good housekeeping starts at home, my boy. A tight ship is a happy ship. So listen sharp! Any loose talk, any hint of disloyalty, any breath of false rumor against the good name of the Tri-Mutual Guaranteed Trust and Loan . . . report it to me. Understand?"

"Yes, sir, Mr. Briggs," said Nick. "I'll keep my ear peeled."

"Good boy," said the banker with a grin. "I knew I had your number. I'll let you out after hours and we'll have another chat."

"But my lunch . . . !"

"Didn't you bring it with you? Oh, no matter. I'll pass you in a sandwich around noontime." The banker started to close the door.

"But I told my father I'd be home at noon. . . ."

"As a businessman himself, he will understand," said the banker, closing the door and locking it from the outside.

When Nick's eyes had become accustomed to the darkness, he saw the two tiny rays of light described by his employer. By applying his eye to one and then the other, our hero determined that the peepholes had been cleverly placed so as to provide a very comprehensive view of the chambers in question. At this hour, of course, they were unoccupied.

"Gosh," whispered Nick to himself, as he realized the

nature of his duties, so different from what he had expected, "this is *something!*" I am sure my young readers
will understand his excitement, for Nick was in the en-
viable position of realizing the dreams of every American
boy, while being paid for it at the same time. "Golly
gee!" he whispered, taking a second look through his
peepholes.

I perhaps should remind my young readers that at the
time of which I am writing (which was before the
fame that attended Mr. Hoover and his redoubtable
"G-men," who have acquitted themselves so well in the
ongoing war against crime) the Pinkerton Men were
achieving miracles of detection and law enforcement,
their well-known emblem of alert surveillance the cyno-
sure of every red-blooded American eye. Nick was no
exception to the rule, and with others of his age and
interests, he had eagerly devoured the true case histories
compiled by that assiduous penman, Allan Pinkerton.

For though his father was adamant concerning the consumption of dime novels and the like worthless fictional
trash by his sons, he approved the reading of more
healthy, factual material, and from time to time loaned his
sons volumes from his own small and carefully closeted
library, as a special reward for diligence and application.

"If a Pinkerton Man ran for President," he was wont
to say, "I'd cross party lines to vote for him."

"Is that legal?" asked Obie.

"What Father means," explained Nick, "is that true
worth transcends mere political labels."

"Law and Order," said Mr. Noxin, "know no party."
These generous sentiments were typical of the Western
spirit, the state which was Mr. Noxin's chosen abode
being known for its cross-ticket candidates.

So it was that Nick had a worthy model in mind as he
applied himself to his new job, watching through this
hole first, then that, and straining his ear so that no scrap
of conversation would escape him. He soon learned that
detective work is often monotonous, and there were dull
interludes in his closet, long stretches between conversations, nor was the atmosphere of the cramped space always pleasant to Nick's olfactory sense. And, it must be
said, much of what he witnessed that day was trite and
unimportant, of no value to his employer or himself and
certainly not to my young reader, whom I shall not bore
by recording what took place in the washrooms.

Indeed, the only conversation worth repeating occurred
on the other side of Nick's closet, in the banker's office,
and was overheard by our hero during his lunch break,
as he sat eating a jelly sandwich, the bread of which was
toasted stale. But let us save the intriguing details of
that conversation for the following chapter, which begins
the next installment of the adventures of Nick Noxin,
Boy Detective.

CHAPTER VIII

What Nick Heard
and
What Happened Next

🖝

Numerous conversations had taken place in Banker Briggs's office during the course of the morning, mostly muffled and sonorous, and our young detective often had to plug one ear with his finger as he placed the other against the washroom wall. But this discussion was louder than all others, and though Nick tried hard not to listen —that was not, after all, what he was being paid to do, and he was enjoying his lunch break, besides—he could not help but catch many of the words, nor was he able to ignore the certainty that one of the voices was that of Squire Farley, of Farley Farms, who was, it seemed, exchanging increasingly heated remarks with Nick's employer.

"Curse you, Aeneas Briggs!" swore the furious Squire.
"How do you expect me to make a profit when you send
me Chinks who don't know a bean from a . . ." The
last word was unintelligible to Nick, as were others
which were said, but the general drift of the argument
was as follows:

"That's no concern of mine," said the banker. "I am
accountable to my board, and, quite frankly, your profits
are nil. Therefore I cannot see my way clear to extending your note. Money is tight these days, you know."

"Note? Why you old [unintelligible word], you didn't
call it a *note* when you loaned me the money!"

"You should have read what you were signing," said
the banker. "The note comes due tomorrow, and I shall
have to call it in."

"That means I'll be ruined!" cried the agonized Squire.

"That's not my responsibility," said the banker calmly.
"Business is business, profit or loss."

"Your profit and my loss, hey? Ha ha ha ha!" laughed
the Squire, bitterly. "Well, Briggs, there's different kinds
of *business,* ain't there? And your business stinks to high
heaven!"

"You were glad to take the money when I loaned it
to you," said the banker. "And as for profit and loss, I
could never make much money if all my clients were im-
provident deadbeats."

"Deadbeat, is it? I know your game, Briggs. You've
been watching the calf fatten, and now you're going to

slaughter it. I've poured thousands into that farm. Thousands! And you're planning to get it by recalling your note. . . ."

"What poppycock!" said the banker. "The property will go to the highest bidder, that's the rule of a bankruptcy auction."

"I know all about you and your auctions, Briggs. You won't get away with this. Nobody ever made a goat out of *me*. I'm blowing the whistle on this whole operation. Is that clear?"

"Don't make me laugh, Farley," said the banker. "If guts were dynamite, you couldn't [unintelligible words]. Now get out of here before I have you thrown out. You're finished!"

"Aw, I was only joking, Aeneas," whined the Squire. "Give me a break, will you? A second chance. I'd do as much for you . . . !"

"Yes, you probably would, you lily-livered [unintelligible word], but I didn't get where I am today by giving anybody second chances."

"But think of my fa-family. My da-darling wuh-wife and dear buh-boy?"

"Stop your sniveling, Farley. I just ate lunch. As for that charmless, lazy brat of yours, you can tell him for me that his period of employment here has ended. I've found a much more dependable and *grateful* replacement. . . ."

"Oh, little Frank is *very* grateful, Aeneas. He blesses

you in his prayers every night. But, as I've explained, he has a terrible heat rash. . . . Any exertion in this weather . . ."

"The best cure for heat rash is more heat, Farley. Right on the old aspidistra obbligato."

"I believe," said Squire Farley, "that I'm the best judge of that."

"You? You couldn't judge a turtle race. Now get out!"

"The old heave-ho, hey? Well, you just wait, Aeneas Briggs! Nobody kicks Alphonse Farley around and gets away with it!"

At this point the sound of flushing waters drowned the rest of the conversation, and Nick swallowed the remainder of his sandwich. He had hardly a moment to reflect on the meaning of what he had overheard when the sound of a key in the lock interrupted his thoughts, and a moment later the door opened, letting in a flood of light only partially blocked by the dark shadow of his employer.

"You heard all that, I assume?" the banker demanded.

"Oh no, sir," said Nick. "I was eating my lunch. Very tasty."

"That fool Farley has a big mouth," growled Aeneas Briggs. "I never should have had anything to do with him."

"I wouldn't know anything about it," said Nick. "I was . . ."

"Don't try to con me, Noxin," said the banker. "I'm the man you work for, remember?"

"Oh, sir," said Nick, "I . . ."

"Now listen sharp, Noxin. You heard Farley putting the bite on me to extend his loan, didn't you?"

"Well," said Nick, "he . . ."

"Right you are!" said the banker. "You heard *threats*, didn't you? A raised voice? Personal abuse? And after all I've done for him and that worthless brat of his . . . !"

"Did Frank . . . ?"

"You see what I mean about enemies, Noxin. A man like Farley, whom I picked up off the street, practically, and gave a new start, a chance to make something of himself, and now he turns on me. The unmitigated gall . . . !"

"Tch, tch!" said our hero.

"Disloyalty! How I hate it! But don't worry, Noxin, that traitor will pay for it, if he tries anything, which I doubt he will. I'll need your help, of course."

"I'll be glad to do . . ."

"Good. You can start by forgetting everything you've heard for now. If I need you to bear witness, I'll tell you what to say, is that understood?"

"Oh, yes, *sir!*" said Nick.

"Good. Let's get back to work. What do you think of the banking business *now,* Noxin?"

"Well," said Nick, "it's certainly different from what I expected."

"Exciting stuff, Noxin. Keeps a man on his toes. The adventure of big business, there's nothing like it. Makes Monopoly look like child's play. Survival of the fittest,

my boy! If Farley makes any trouble, we'll cut him off at
the knees!"

"I can hardly wait!" cried our hero, pleased to be ad-
mitted to the banker's confidence so early in his period
of employ.

Later that day, Nick was let out of his office by Mr.
Briggs, and spent the closing hours of the afternoon re-
counting what he had heard in the washrooms. None of
that information bears on the events of our story, so I
shall not pester my young reader with it, but hasten on
instead to the Friday following, which was to prove very
eventful indeed for our Boy Detective.

Early in the morning, as usual, Nick ran down to
Bragadura Cove, but for once he did not practice his
oratory. As he was nearing the beach, a police officer
stepped out from behind a tree and stopped him.

"Where you running to, kid?"

"My name is Nicholas Noxin," said our hero stoutly,
having nothing to fear from the Law, "and I'm going
for a swim."

"Not today you're not. Nobody goes near that beach.
Chief's orders."

"Bragadura Cove," said Nick, "is a public area, I believe."

"That's right, kid. And I'm a public cop, and if you
don't turn around and get moving, I'll turn you in for
a public nuisance. Hop!"

"I shall be glad to obey any lawful order, officer," said
Nick.

"Don't give me none of your lip," said the policeman, speeding him on his way with a heavy boot. "I hate sarcastic kids."

Nick, of course, had no intention of visiting the beach that day, and bore no resentment against the officer, who was only doing his duty. But it did appear as though somebody's suspicions had been raised by Mr. Alibi's unorthodox business habits, and Nick was therefore doing *his* duty by obeying the policeman's lawful command, thus meriting the trust put in him by his generous, if quixotic, employer.

Later that same day our hero had occasion to merit the trust of his other, equally unorthodox employer, Mr. Briggs, for early in the afternoon the door to Nick's office was opened suddenly, cutting him off in the middle of a conversation and nearly blinding him.

"Yes, sir, Mr. Briggs, sir?" said Nick, rising and blinking.

"Time for our little trip, my boy," said the banker, handing our hero an empty straw suitcase of an inexpensive design.

"I shall welcome the diversion," said Nick, "but isn't it rather late in the day?"

"*Late?* Do you call two o'clock late?"

"Well, if I have to go all the way to Long Beach, it will be after dark before I get back."

"Does the grass stop growing because the sun goes down?" asked the banker. "No, it doesn't, and we don't want it growing under our feet, do we?"

"No, sir," said Nick. "I shall leave immediately."

"That's the spirit, my boy. Here are the tickets, round-trip."

"Won't I need the address of the Charity Bazaar?" asked Nick.

"What? Don't be silly! Why would you need that?"

"I am to pick up the receipts there, am I not?"

"No, no!" cried the banker. "You're to do no such thing! Not on *any* account. Avoid the place like the plague! That is," he added more calmly, "you won't have to. Won't have time, I mean. Besides, I have enemies, if you'll recall. You'll be watched at all times. Stay on your toes. Keep alert."

"Oh, I shall," said Nick. "But why would a charity bazaar have enemies?"

"Why indeed?" said the banker. "That's a good question, a very good question. Why does a dog have fleas? A sign of the moral decline of the nation, I should say. But time is money, my boy, and money waits for no man. The point is to be careful every step of the way. When you get off the train in Long Beach, go straight into the station and sit down on the bench under the clock. A redheaded man will sit down next to you. When he leaves, take the suitcase he will exchange for this one, and return on the next train. Call me before you leave, and I will meet you at the station. You have your tickets. Any questions?"

"What will I do for supper?" asked Nick.

"Is that all you think about, *food?*" snapped the banker.

"Well, I am a growing boy," said Nick.

"Don't worry," said Mr. Briggs. "I've packed an apple in the suitcase. Anything else?"

"No, sir," said Nick.

"I suppose it may seem to you a strange way to conduct business," said the banker with a smile. "I imagine you're wondering why I don't send the receipts through more conventional channels."

"No, sir," said Nick. "I'm not being paid to wonder."

"Spoken like a boy after my own heart!" crowed the banker. "Mum's the word, hey?" Closing one eye, he placed a finger next to his nose. "Secrecy is of the essence, Nicholas. It's the unwritten word in the Bill of Rights. The Right to . . . *Secrecy!* Most sacred Secrecy, without which the machinery of our great Republic, and the economic system for which it stands, would shudder to a halt!"

Our hero shuddered likewise. "Horrible!" he said.

"Right you are. Thank the Lord for Secrecy. You see, my boy, there are some people who might draw unfavorable conclusions as to the nature of my many good works from the methods I use, which are, admittedly, unorthodox. My enemies, for example, by which I am surrounded. You have no idea, Nicholas, how much I am hated in this town. Such is the price of power. So I am forced to employ these unorthodox methods in order to protect myself, and that is why I cannot send the money through regular banking channels. Oh," he concluded, raising his eyes and hands, "if only I could! My life would be so much simpler."

"But then," said Nick, "I wouldn't have a job."

"True, true," said the banker. "It's an ill wind that blows no good."

"Well, your secrets are safe with me, sir," said our hero. "I shall act in all ways so as to avoid suspicion."

"Spoken like a true banker!" chortled Mr. Briggs. "And now, off with you, my boy. Don't forget to call, person-to-person and collect, naturally, And be careful, Nicholas. Trust no one."

"Don't worry, sir," said Nick, heading for the door. "I . . ."

"Not out that way, you idiot!" cried the banker. "Can't you do anything right without first being told?"

"I . . . I wasn't aware that there was a second door," stammered Nick, looking hastily about.

"Who said there was?" asked the banker, opening his window and peering up and down the alley. "Out this way, and make it snappy. Remember, Noxin, keep alert. When things seem clearest, the ice is thinnest."

"He who . . ." began Nick, as he clambered out the window.

"Hurry along, now," said the banker, helping our hero along with a blow from a steel ruler. "I don't pay you to sit on windowsills reciting aphorisms all day!"

Picking himself up and dusting himself off, Nick moved quickly to the opening at the far end of the alley. Then, having looked up and down the street, he turned toward the railway station a few blocks away.

The platform was empty, which was quite normal for Poco Lobo, and the stationmaster was asleep, but at that very moment a train pulled into the station with a loud clanging of its bell and a discharge of steam and cinders. A conductor leaned out and shouted, "Anaheim, Azuza, Cucamonga . . . and Looong Beach!"

"I'm in luck!" said Nick, running for the train and scampering aboard. For the next half hour he sat contemplating the limited view afforded from his open window (this being before the days of modern, air-conditioned cars), amusing himself by trying to decipher the words of the faded cigar advertisement on the side of the Poco Lobo Old Mission Inn, but at last the train began to move, and a cool breeze fanned his moist brow and upper lip.

But then, as the train pulled out of the station, Nick noticed a small figure standing in the shadow of the platform canopy. He quickly recognized the familiar, sneering features of Frank Farley, who waved as Nick's car moved past.

"Have a nice trip, grocersboy!" he shouted. "See you when you get back!"

—Hm, wondered Nick, who was beginning to be affected by his employer's suspicions. —I wonder what he meant by that?

The novelty of his new situation, however, soon put thoughts of Frank Farley out of his mind, and our hero sat back in his seat to enjoy the view, as the afternoon sunlight stained the California hills a rich golden color, perfectly in harmony with his propects and hence with his mood.

CHAPTER IX

A
Train Ride

☛

Nick was interrupted in his reverie by the conductor, who asked for his ticket. "Long Beach?" asked that officious agent of the Southern Pacific, upon examining the object in question, "Why didn't you take the express? Due in ten minutes after we pulled out."

"Well," said Nick, "can't I change at the next sta . . . ?"

He was interrupted by a rattling roar outside his window, as a blur of speeding cars shot past, giving him the impression that he was actually moving backwards, which, in a relative sense, he was.

"Nope," said the conductor, after the roar had passed. "That was it, straight through to Long Beach."

"Well," said Nick. "I like to take in the view."

"Help yourself," said the conductor, who, like many of

his kind, fancied himself a wit. "There's lots of it, what there *is* of it." Having punched Nick's ticket, he moved on down the aisle.

Nick sat back in his seat once again and looked out the open window, occasionally blinking as a cinder lodged in his eye, but otherwise studying the California country-side, the long, orderly rows of orchards, vineyards, and vegetable gardens, not unlike those in which he had nar-rowly missed spending his summer. But all that was be-hind him now, and Nick smiled to himself as he thought of the opportunities which the generosity of Aeneas Briggs had opened to him.

Others might hate the old banker, but not Nick, nor did our hero question the eccentric procedures used by his employer, saving his suspicions for the enemies of the man who befriended him. —I must stay alert, he said to himself. Putting his words into practice, he looked about the car, and noticed for the first time a man sitting across the aisle, facing backwards so as to watch him.

—An enemy, and not yet to Anaheim! A thrill shivered our hero's spine, but summoning all his courage, Nick gave the man stare for stare, for such was the stuff of which he was made.

During this resolute exchange, Nick had the oppor-tunity to study the appearance of the stranger across the way, and his impressions were decidedly not in the man's favor. Of a roseate complexion, suggesting a bibulous disposition, the man was dressed in a shabbily flashy manner, wearing a threadbare, candy-striped blazer and ice-cream trousers that bagged at the knee. His flowing, lemon-sateen cravat was fixed with a glittering stickpin, decorated with either a diamond or a rhinestone, though nothing about the man suggested that the former was even a remote possibility.

The stranger's eyes were a watery blue, rimmed with red, and were suited to the general dissoluteness of his other features, his puffy cheeks and bulbous, nearly purple nose. Everything about this seedy-looking individual aroused Nick's distrust, and he was not all pleased when the stranger doffed his dingy Panama and smiled at him.

"Ah, young man," said the stranger, rising with a nasal wheeze of strained cordiality. "May I join you?"

Reluctant as he was to accept this intrusion on his privacy, Nick was too well-bred a boy to do otherwise. "I don't own this train," he said with a shrug, at the same time taking a tight hold on the handle of his suitcase.

Sitting down across from Nick, the red-faced man made himself quickly at ease. "Nice day," he observed, a simpleminded statement which Nick acknowledged with the silence it deserved. "But then it's always a nice day in California."

"That depends on the circumstances," observed Nick pointedly.

"Well put, well put!" said the stranger with a laugh. "Let us improve them, shall we?" Removing a worn wallet from his inner coat pocket, the red-faced man took out an equally worn bit of pasteboard which he held out

for Nick's inspection. "Allow me to introduce myself,"
he said, letting the card perform that service.

Q. DIGBY PITT (it read)
INVESTMENT COUNSELOR EXTRODINARY
19 LA BREA BLVD., LOS ANGELES, CALIFORNIA

The misspelling which Nick's alert eye immediately
detected did nothing to encourage his confidence in the
man, nor did the fact that, having displayed his card to
our hero, the stranger returned it to his wallet, for the
action suggested that he could only spare the loan and
not the permanent entrusting of his identity.

"And what," pressed the stranger, "is your name, young
man?"

"Thomas A. Edison," said Nick, for our hero was not
without a sense of humor when the occasion called for
one.

"Is that right? My, my, you have been blessed with a
fortunate cognomen! May I ask where you are going,
Master Edison?"

"Certainly," said Nick. "You just did."

"Ah, yes. . . . So I did, didn't I? And where *are* you
going?"

"To Peru," said Nick. "To visit my great-uncle. He
owns half of the country and he's dying of stomach can-
cer."

"A sobering thought," observed the roseate stranger,
paling to a light shade of pink.

"Yes," said Nick. "I haven't had a drink for days."

"Speaking of which," said Mr. Digby Pitt, "it's time for my heart medicine." Taking a small flask from his coat pocket, which appeared to be nickel-plated but may indeed have been silver, he unscrewed the top and drank deeply from it. "Aaaah!" he sighed, lowering the flask as tears rolled down his cheeks. "Keeps the old ticker ticking."

"To each his own," observed Nick, not at all fooled by the ruse.

"Speaking of which," said Mr. Pitt, replacing the flask and removing a thin case of the same metal, "Do you care to join me in a smoke?"

"No," said Nick firmly, "I do not care to."

"Do you mind if I smoke, then, Master Edison? Or do they call you 'Tom'?"

"I can't stop you," said Nick, "and they call me 'Alva.' "

"You know, Alva," said Mr. Pitt, having struck a match on the upholstery and ignited his cigarette, "I *like* you."

"So do I," said Nick. "That's why I don't smoke."

"Admirable, most admirable," said Mr. Pitt, blowing a cloud of smoke discreetly to one side. "I regret that I ever took up the habit, I can assure you. A vile pastime, consuming time and money better spent in more profitable and healthful activities. Fortunately," he added with a smile, "I am without dependents and in quite comfortable circumstances, quite comfortable indeed. I am," said Mr. Pitt with a wink, "a billionaire!"

"So is my uncle," said Nick, who was hard put not to laugh aloud.

"But you, of course, are not."

"Not yet," said Nick.

"Perhaps I can be of some service, in any event," said Mr. Pitt. "You see," he went on earnestly, leaning forward and placing two fingers lightly on our hero's knee, on which the stones of two large rings flashed gaudily, "I am involved in frequent stock-market deals, where the right word in the right place can make or break a fortune."

"Is that right?" said Nick, shifting his knee.

"Only last week, in fact, I parlayed ten dollars given me by a newspaperboy, to whom I had taken a fancy—you remind me of him, by the way—into ten thousand dollars. That money is now invested in solid, blue-chip stock, and by the time the boy comes of age, he will take over a tidy fortune."

"Is that right?" said Nick, folding his legs under him.

"Had the boy entrusted twenty dollars to me, I could of course have done much better by him."

"Is that right?" said Nick, wondering whether he should be angry with this man for thinking him such a fool as to believe his ridiculous story or feel sorry for him because of his own simplicity.

"Indeed it is. And little acts like that bring light and happiness into my gloomy bachelor life."

"Cheap at the price, I guess," observed Nick.

"Now," said Mr. Pitt, leaning forward and lowering his voice to a confidential whisper, "how much could you spare, Master Edison?"

"Gosh," said Nick. "All I have is enough to get me to Peru."

"Come, come," said Mr. Pitt, his smile fading. 'Surely you aren't going to persist in that silly tale about a dying uncle?"

"Do you have a *better* one?" asked Nick, pointedly.

"Then you don't believe me?"

"That's the general idea," said Nick.

"I see," said Mr. Pitt with a sigh. "Distrust." He rose with a shake of his head. "America was not built on skepticism, you know."

"Nor do promises fill my purse," said Nick.

"I wish you every success possible based on such a cynical philosophy," said the red-faced Mr. Pitt. Drawing his unshapely body as stiffly erect as he could manage, he left the car in search of some more grateful recipient of his generosity.

"Huh!" snorted Nick. "Good riddance to bad rubbish."

"HERE YA ARE! PEANUT, CANDY, CRACKER-JACK! GETCHER FRESH FRUIT HERE! JUST IN FROM FLORIDA! PEANUT, CANDY, CRACKER-JACK!"

Nick turned in his seat to find a candy butcher, a boy not much older than himself, lugging a huge basket of comestibles and cheap railroad literature down the aisle. The sight of all that food made Nick's mouth water.

"HERE YA ARE!" bawled the butcher, a stocky lad

whose pimply face suggested that he often indulged in his own wares. "GETCHER CANDY HERE! LAST CALL FER PEANUT, CANDY, CRACKERJACK! PRIZE IN EVERY BOX SO WATCH WHATCHER EATIN'! FRESH FRUIT! LATEST MAGAZINES! *CAPTAIN BILLY'S WHIZBANG,* JUST OFF THE PRESS!" Noticing Nick's interest, the voluble boy stopped by his seat so as to let our hero view the contents of his veritable cornucopia. "Hi, bub!" he said enthusiastically. "Anything here you can use?"

"Yes," said Nick, unwilling to let the boy think he could not afford something from the basket. "I guess I'll take a licorice stick."

"Crimineys! A whole stick!"

"Yes," said Nick, blushing visibly as he reached for his coin purse. "I have just finished a big dinner and it will help my digestion."

"Is that right?" asked the candy butcher, exchanging a black twist of the confection in question for Nick's hard-earned penny. "Don't tell anybody where you got it, then. I don't have a license to sell medicine." Putting the coin into the pocket of his apron, the stocky boy sat down on the arm of the chair across the aisle and let out a sigh. "Well," he announced, "guess I'll cool my tootsies for a minute. Where you heading, 'Country'?"

Nick winced at the implication. "New York City," he said.

"From Long Beach?"

"I'm taking the boat," said Nick. "My uncle's boat."

"Say," said the butcher, helping himself to a candy bar, "he must be plenty rich."

"I should say so," said Nick, pleased at the effect of his announcement. So as to make the candy butcher more comfortable in his presence, for he seemed like a friendly if somewhat coarse young man, Nick changed the subject. "Tell me," he began, "how's Babe Ruth doing these days? I've been out of the country."

"Aw, Hershey outsells 'em two to one," said the butcher, crumpling up his candy wrapper and shooting it past Nick's nose out the open window. "And that's a fact."

"No," said Nick. "I mean the ball player."

"Gee, he's doin' okay, I guess. Hey, if your uncle is rich, I'll bet he knows Q. Digby Pitt. . . ."

"Who?" asked Nick, startled by the name.

"The Eccentric Billionaire, you *know*. Always up to some crazy stunt. Ever meet him?"

"I . . . I wouldn't know," said Nick.

"Yeh? Well he's right on this train, and that's a fact. I saw him get on at Santa Barbara. That's where he lives, you know. He was all rigged out in drummer's clothes, but I recognized him from his pitchers."

"Is that right?" asked Nick.

"A fact. I guess he must be in one of the cars up ahead, though. I haven't come across him yet. Well," said the butcher, picking up his basket again, "gotta get marchin'. Who knows, maybe he'll take a shine ta me an' give me

a few hot tips on the market. I see in the papers last week
where he made some lucky kid ten thou on a ten buck
loan. Set him up fer life."

"Is that right?" asked Nick.

"Fact. Seen it in the papers," said the boy, shouldering
his strap. "Well, keep yer fingers crossed, bub. Maybe
he'll give *you* a break, ya never know. 'Course, I guess
you don't *need* it."

"No," said Nick, the licorice stick growing gummy in
his clenched fist. "I guess not."

"Well, wish me luck, Country. HERE YA ARE!
CANDY, PEANUT, CRACKERJACK! THEY AIN'T
GETTIN' NO FRESHER WHILE YA MAKE UP YER
MIND! CANDY, PEANUT, CRACKERJACK!"

Pushing through the door into the next car with his
back, the pimply butcher gave Nick a final grin and a
wink, which our hero returned with as much pep as he
was able to summon.

We will leave him for the moment to his own thoughts,
the most consoling if least convincing of which was that
the fraud in the striped coat and the candy butcher were
confederates in a league of swindlers. Nick took his re-
venge on the latter by peeling back the wrapper on a bar
of candy that he had snitched from the boy's basket.

"Better safe than sorry," he reflected sagely if somewhat
sourly, biting into his purloined sweets as he did so and
partway through his tongue.

Chapter X

Auld
Acquaintance
and
Some New

Later that afternoon, Nick found himself in the busy Long Beach station, and made his way to the passenger bench under the clock, as Banker Briggs had instructed. There were no empty places on the bench, but Nick's sharp eyes quickly picked out the red-haired gentleman mentioned by the banker. He was asleep, his red hair having slipped forward over his face. Next to him on the bench was a straw suitcase with leather straps, identical to the one Nick carried, its handle fastened to the man's wrist with a metal chain.

"Excuse me, sir," said Nick, touching the man's arm. "Is this seat . . . ?"

"Whuzzat?" cried the gentleman, sitting abruptly upright, and reaching inside his jacket. This precipitous action caused his red wig to fall into his lap, and Nick quickly recognized the dark features of his old acquaintance, Mr. Alibi.

"Mr. Alibi!" he cried, surprised at this unexpected revelation.

"Well, well," said that gentleman, quickly recovering himself. "What brings you to Long Beach, son?"

"I . . . I have a new job," said Nick. "I mean *another* job. I would have told you, but you haven't been to . . . I haven't seen you lately."

"Yeh," said Mr. Alibi. "It's been kind of *hot* this past week. I'm thinking of taking a little cruise for my health." Picking up his wig, he put it back on his head, and looked past Nick, his eyes moving this way and that as he surveyed the passersby.

"I imagine that will cost a great deal of *money*," said Nick, lifting his suitcase and holding it in both his arms.

"Yes," said Mr. Alibi. "More than you know." He continued to look about, and failed to notice Nick's suitcase.

"What brings *you* to Long Beach?" asked our hero, resolutely moving this way and that so as to bring the suitcase to Mr. Alibi's attention.

"Business," said that tawny individual. "Same as you."

"The *same as I*, you said?"

"Yes, that's what I said. Are you deaf?" Mr. Alibi seemed to be growing impatient over Nick's persistence.

"But why would you be conducting business *under the clock in the Long Beach Railway Station?*" asked Nick pointedly. "I thought you liked your privacy."

"Believe me, bud," said Mr. Alibi, "there's nothing like a crowd for absolute privacy. But I would like to be *alone,* if you get my meaning. . . ."

"But why are you wearing that *red wig?*" persisted Nick.

"My other one is at the cleaners," said Mr. Alibi, whose irritation was becoming visible. "Look, bud, why don't you go over to the staircase there and look up the ladies' skirts?"

Nick blushed visibly and dropped his suitcase on Mr. Alibi's toe. "Oops!" he stammered. "I dropped my *straw suitcase* on your toe."

"Yeh you did," said Mr. Alibi, grimly. "Good thing it was empty." Lifting the foot in question, he none too gently dusted off his shoe on the seat of Nick's new trousers.

"I'll bet *your* suitcase isn't empty," said Nick. "It looks *very heavy.*"

"You're right," said Mr. Alibi. "There's a nosy kid in there."

"Why is it *chained to your wrist?*" asked Nick, growing desperate.

"So he won't *get lost,*" growled Mr. Alibi. "But don't let that stop *you.*"

"What do you know!" cried Nick, who had begun to perspire heavily. *"You have a straw suitcase just like mine!"*

"So I do," said Mr. Alibi, looking for the first time at Nick's.

"One of those coincidences, I guess," said our hero. "Like our meeting under the clock in the Long Beach Railway Station."

"Yeh. Have a seat, son," said Mr. Alibi, lifting his own suitcase off the bench to make room. "Take a load off your Buster Browns."

"How did you know . . . ?"

"I'm a shoe salesman in civilian life," said Mr. Alibi. "Well, it's been great talking to you, bud. I gotta see a man about a horse."

Rising, Mr. Alibi took Nick's empty suitcase and hurried off, losing himself quickly in the crowded station. Our hero quickly fastened the chain about his own wrist, and after waiting a decent interval, got to his feet once again, which were (it must be said) sorely troubled by the sharp-toed bargains.

The weight of the suitcase did not make walking any easier, either, but Nick manfully hobbled over to the information counter and waited in line for more than an hour, the onerousness of his ordeal increased by his being shoved aside by older people each time he reached the counter. But finally he caught the agent's eye by waving his straw hat in the air.

"When does the next express leave for Poco Lobo?" he asked.

"There's no express for Poco Lobo," said the agent. "You have to change to the local at Santa Barbara."

"Well, then," said Nick patiently. "When does the next express leave for Santa Barbara?"

"It just did," said the agent, turning away.

"WAIT! WAIT!" cried Nick in desperation. "How about the *next* next express . . . ?"

"There isn't any," said the man. "Not until tomorrow. But the Cucamonga, Azuza, Anaheim and Poco Lobo local is loading now on Platform Five. You'd better hustle, unless you want to take the trolley car to San Fernando."

"San Fernando?" asked Nick. "How do I get to Poco Lobo from there?"

"You can't," said the man, laughing loudly. "That's why you'd better hustle!"

He was joined in this laughter at our hero's expense by the rude throng around the counter, who were cruelly indifferent to Nick's plight. Clenching his jaw, Nick took up his heavy suitcase once again and limped to a pay phone, where he placed a call to Mr. Briggs, as instructed.

"I'm leaving Long Beach now," he said, as soon as his employer answered.

"What I want to know," said the banker peevishly, "is when you're due to *arrive*."

"I . . . I forgot to ask, sir," said Nick. "But it's the last train to Poco Lobo, and if I don't hustle, I'll have to spend the night in Long Beach."

"Well, *hustle* then! I'm not paying you to stand around making expensive long-distance calls!"

"Yes, sir," said Nick, hanging up the receiver and picking up his bag once again.

Our hero made it to the train just in time, and when

he climbed into the last car he found that it was filled
with passengers, the aisles crowded with luggage and
shopping parcels. But at the far end he saw an empty
place, so lugging his heavy suitcase and hobbled by his
tight shoes, Nick pushed his way through the aisle only
to find the seat occupied by a small child.

Our hero was nonetheless thankful that he had managed to get aboard, and making his way to the very end
of the swaying car, he sat down on his suitcase. Anything
was preferable to standing.

"What do you think you're doing?" asked the conductor, who came through just at that moment.

"Here," said Nick, holding out his ticket.

"That entitles you to a *seat*," growled the irritated
petty official. "It doesn't mean you can block the aisle."

"I am hardly the only one doing so," said Nick, pointedly pointing to the various parcels and suitcases, and
receiving a number of angry scowls from their owners.

"Two wrongs don't make a right," said the conductor.
"I'm taking about *you*, not them!"

"You are picking on me," said Nick, defiantly remaining where he was. "Because I'm a small boy, you think
you can shove me around. Well, I know my rights . . . !"

"Rights, hey?" cried the conductor, growing red in the
face. Picking Nick up by the scruff of his no longer natty
Palm-Beach suitcoat, he headed for the door. "You may
be *right*, kid, but you're gonna be *left* . . . !"

At that moment the chain on Nick's wrist brought the
conductor up short, the heavy suitcase serving as an

anchor, much to the amusement of the passengers, who had been watching the argument with unconcealed delight, none of them being involved in it.

This only served to inflame the conductor's passions, and despite Nick's cries of discomfort, he continued to pull our hero toward the door, the suitcase dragging along behind.

"HOLD ON THERE, CONDUCTOR!" cried a stern voice out of the general laughter. "UNHAND THAT LAD!"

The authoritative command made the conductor stop and turn about, thus enabling Nick to view his benefactor, who was a tall, blond, and blue-eyed man with a deep tan and white smile. "What's it to you, mister?" snarled the mean-spirited official.

"The boy has bought his ticket and may sit next to me," said the man. "The place is improperly occupied with luggage belonging to this gentleman across the aisle."

"And what am I supposed to do with the luggage?" growled the conductor.

"That is your responsibility," said the blond man, rising up and depositing the luggage in the aisle, "for which you are amply compensated, I believe."

As he straightened up, the kind stranger revealed to our hero a small golden cross that was fixed in the lapel of his dark blue suit, a revelation shared by the conductor, who quickly changed his tune.

"Sure, Reverend," he said, setting Nick on his feet gently. "I'll take care of it right away. Here, *you*," he growled to the red-faced man across the aisle, who now was receiving the scowls of the passengers. "What do you mean taking up a seat with your luggage? Don't you read the regulations?"

Picking up the suitcases, the conductor shoved them roughly under the legs of the uncomfortable passenger, forcing him to assume a very awkward position, much to the delight of those of his fellow passengers who were without extra luggage. To the relief of the remainder, the conductor refrained from imposing similar discomforts, and merely passed through the car asking for tickets.

At the kind stranger's insistence, Nick took the window seat, so he could catch the full benefit of the setting sun as it dropped beneath the rolling California hills.

"Thank you, sir," said Nick, gratefully.

"Was it not written, 'Suffer the little children' . . . ?"

"I'm not exactly a little child," said Nick, "but I've certainly been suffering."

"That's not quite the meaning of the text," said the man of God with a smile. "Are you, perhaps, of the Hebrew persuasion?"

"Oh no," said Nick, visibly blushing, "I'm a Friend."

"You needn't be embarrassed," said the minister. "I have acquaintances who are Friends, though I happen to be a Methodist. You see, I believe in tolerance of *all* faiths, great and small."

"Oh so do I," said Nick. "I even work for an Episcopalian."

"You seem rather young for regular employment," said the Methodist.

"I am spending the summer learning the banking business from Mr. Briggs, of the Tri-Mutual Guaranteed Trust and Loan, in Poco Lobo."

"I have heard of Mr. Briggs. An estimable gentleman. I have a number of acquaintances in Poco Lobo, as a matter of fact.

"My father's name is Noxin," said Nick. "Do you know *him?*"

"Toxin? That does ring a bell," said the Methodist, thoughtfully.

"No, *Noxin,*" said Nick. "Norman O. Noxin—Groceries and Gas."

"I'm sure that I've met him," said the Methodist. "My name is Xenophon T. Peachy. Be sure to give him my regards."

"My name is Nicholas," said our hero. "But my friends call me 'Nick.' "

"And I'll bet you have some of the old 'Nick' in you, too!" said the Methodist, with a wink and a nudge.

"Oh," said Nick. "No more than any normal American boy."

"You won't believe me," said the Methodist, "but I was quite a devil when I was your age. I used to chase the girls every chance I got. Even at Sunday-School Picnics. What do you think of *that?*"

"I . . . I'm not sure," said Nick, somewhat baffled by the strange turn of conversation.

"Oh, yes. I'd chase them into the woods. Then," he said, lowering his voice and leaning toward Nick's ear, "and then we'd . . ."

"Say!" said Nick. "Who else do you know in Poco Lobo?"

"Poco Lobo?" asked Reverend Peachy, sitting abruptly erect and chewing his lower lip in thought. "Let me see. . . ." He rolled his eyes up toward the ceiling. "Name some names."

"How about Phineas T. Thatcher?"

"Sounds familiar. What does he do?"

"Runs the hardware store with his brother."

"Oh, yes! Phineas T. Thatcher. A fine man, a Christian gentleman. I know him well, and his brother, too, old . . . whats-his-name."

"Bill," said Nick.

"Yes, that's right. Old Bill Thatcher. A regular fellow."

"Well," said Nick, "I guess I'll catch a few winks. It's been a long day." Leaning back in his seat and shutting his eyes, our hero sought to terminate the conversation, for the man, whoever he was, was an imposter. Mr. Thatcher's brother was not named William, but Ephraim, and they ran a dry-goods store, not hardware.

"Yes," said the imposter, "I'm rather tired myself. I'll be glad to get back to Santa Barbara."

Nick did his best to keep from falling asleep in fact,

but the gentle rocking of the train car and the steady clicking of the rails had an irresistible effect on him, carrying him to the land of Nod. When he awoke, it was dark outside, and the car was lighted artificially. Peering about with veiled lids, Nick saw to his delight that the man who called himself Xenophon T. Peachy had departed. A stout, rather rugged-looking individual in a derby hat and chewing on a cold cigar butt had taken his place, indeed occupied about one third of Nick's seat as well. But so relieved was our hero at Mr. Peachy's departure that he was glad to accommodate the new passenger.

Opening his eyes, Nick yawned and stretched, and in doing so, noticed that the chain was dangling loose from his wrist.

"Oh my gosh!" he cried, looking desperately about.

"What's wrong?" asked the stout passenger.

"I've lost . . . something," said Nick. "My . . . my suitcase."

"There it is, under your feet! Use your eyes, sonny."

"That's not mine," said Nick. "Mine was straw. The man sitting next to me must have taken it, and left his behind."

"Well, in which case you are ahead in the game. That leather Gladstone must have cost twelve dollars if it cost a dime."

"No," said Nick. "You don't understand. I was carrying . . . Where's the conductor?" Hopping up, our hero looked wildly about.

"Calm down," said the fat man. "He'll be along in a minute."

"Listen, mister," said Nick. "Did you see a tall, good-looking blond man leave the train when you got on? With a cross in his lapel?"

"I got on in Long Beach," said the man. "I've been back in the smoking car. You sure he's the bird who took your bag?"

"I have evidence that he was an imposter," said Nick. "He tried to convince me that he knew Mr. Phineas T. Thatcher, but he didn't."

"Didn't, hey? Those are pretty hard words, son. Think they'll stand up in a court of law?"

"They will if there is such a thing as justice," said Nick, grimly. "But first I've got to catch Mr. Xenophon T. Peachy, for that is the name he gave me, an obvious imposture."

"Sounds like a phony moniker to me, all right," said the man in the derby, reaching into his jacket pocket and pulling out a policeman's badge. "Perhaps I can be of some service."

"You're a policeman?"

"A railroad detective," said the man, putting the badge back.

"Well, what a lucky stroke!" said Nick. "First one today."

"Okay," said the detective. "Describe this jasper to me."

Nick quickly painted a detailed word picture of the

blond imposter, as the detective scribbled notes with a fat fountain pen in a plump, official-looking notebook. "Do you think you can catch him?"

"Does Johnson's make wax?" asked the detective. "If he's still on this train, he's my meat."

"He said he was going all the way to Santa Barbara, now that I think about it."

"Well, here's something else to think about," said the detective, getting up with a grunt. "This train stops in Poco Lobo. The engineer lives there. Now, you stick close to that seat, son, and let me handle this." With brusque efficiency, the fat man made his way out of the car, scrutinizing each passenger as he went.

"Never catch him, not in a million years," said the man across the aisle, whose luggage now sat in the empty seat next to him. "Those sharpies know their stuff. He's probably in Cucamonga, or on his way to someplace else, fast."

"Did he get up when the train stopped at Cucamonga?" asked Nick.

"Maybe. Who knows. It's none of my concern. Kids your age have no business riding on trains unattended. Oughta be a law."

"I'm not a *kid,*" said Nick, resentfully. "I'm a special assistant to Mr. Aeneas Briggs, who runs the Tri-Mutual Trust and Loan Bank, in Poco Lobo."

"You sure that ain't 'Poco Loco'?" asked the nasty man. "Sounds like he oughta have his head examined." With that, he turned in his seat so that his back was facing our hero, nor did anyone else left in the car seem interested in his plight.

Turning to the window, Nick regarded his reflection balefully. What a terrible stroke of bad luck, and all because of a crowded train car. Mr. Briggs would surely fire him for losing all that money intended for his charity work. Nick was all washed up, and not yet turned fourteen. He would be lucky to get a job picking beans.

Nick vowed silently that if fortune would only give him one more chance, just one, when he attained a position of worldly power he would make sure that there were plenty of seats in trains for small boys. He would crack down on the unscrupulous owners of so-called "public" carriers, who packed their cars so full that they became veritable sewers of crime, all in the name of *profit*.

"If I ever get to be Somebody," vowed our hero to himself, "all the trains will run half-empty, and *nobody* will make any profit!"

CHAPTER XI

"Thou Art
the Man!"

☞

Such thoughts consoled our hero for a while, but after the train pulled out of the Anaheim station, Nick began to worry. He also was angry at himself for not getting the detective's name, and began to wonder if perhaps he and Xenophon Peachy were not confederates in league. But why would they waste their time on a mere boy and his cheap straw suitcase?

Suddenly a chill ran up his spine. Why had he not thought of it before? He had been the victim of Mr. Briggs's enemies!

"Laaast stop, Poco Lobooo!" called out the conductor as he passed through the nearly vacated car.

"Conductor!" cried Nick, leaping up. "Do you remember the man who gave me this seat?"

"You're a wise apple, aren't you?" said the conductor.

"One more word out of you, and I'll throw you off this train while it's still moving."

"I have been the victim of a conspiracy against Mr. Briggs, President of the Tri-Mutual Guaranteed Trust and Loan . . . !"

"Then tell it to the police. I've got enough worries as it is," growled the conductor, moving on. "Laaast stop, Poco Lobooo!"

It was with heavy and sore feet that our hero left the train at Poco Lobo, one of a scant half-dozen passengers who quickly hurried off in their various directions. Neither the stout detective nor the thin Mr. Peachy were anywhere to be seen.

Twin headlights blinked at Nick, and taking the leather Gladstone bag in hand, he trudged sadly toward Mr. Briggs's Studebaker. Suddenly a shrill whistle broke the nighttime silence and a half-dozen uniformed men appeared as if from nowhere.

"That's him! That's the kid! Briggs is in the Studebaker!"

"Stop in the name of the law!"

Before Nick could take another step he was seized by strong hands, and the suitcase was wrenched out of his grasp.

"I didn't do anything!" he cried. "I've been robbed!"

"A likely story, Noxin," said a gravelly voice which Nick recognized as that of Police Chief Fred B. Sheibly, of the Poco Lobo constabulary. "We've had our eyes on you for a looong time!"

"I? What have I done?" cried Nick. "The man you want is Xenophon T. Peachy!"

"A likely story," said Police Chief Sheibly.

"Unhand me, you goons!" cried Aeneas Briggs, who to Nick's surprise was brought struggling out of his limousine. "Do you know who I am?"

"The biggest crook in the valley, that's who," said a familiar voice, and Nick turned to see Squire Farley approaching.

"You!" screamed the Banker, expressing Nick's sentiments exactly. "You'll pay for this. You're in it as deep as any of us!"

"Not me," said the Squire with a nasty laugh. "I'm turning State's witness."

"Arrrgh!" cried the Banker, lunging ineffectually against the strong arms which held him back.

"Hold on there!" barked Chief Sheibly. "It is my duty, Mr. Briggs, to warn you that you are resisting a charge of risking arrest. . . . Did I say that right?"

"*Your* duty, you oaf? Who put you where you are?"

"In *ad-dition*," barked the Chief, "to the charge of receiving the revenue of an illegally maintained gambling house under the guise of running a charitable organization."

"I'll bear witness to that!" cried Squire Farley, "And this kid has the loot. Open the Gladstone bag. Your evidence is in there."

Eager fingers tore at the latches and a picklock, deftly inserted, sprung the hasp. The bag was opened and its contents dumped onto the platform: a rather flashy suit of clothes—the sort preferred by drummers—a pair of spats, some soiled underwear, and a sample book.

"What's this?" demanded Chief Sheibly.

"What does it look like?" snapped Banker Briggs. "Dirty clothes. Which I left by mistake in Long Beach, and my employee here has fetched."

"There's been a mistake . . ." began Squire Farley, weakly.

"I'll say there has! Do you know the penalty for pressing a false charge?" cried Chief Sheibly.

"Wait, wait!" cried the Squire. "It's a trick!"

"Right you are," said the Chief. "Grab him, boys. We'll discuss this further in the back room of the station house."

"Bless you, my boy!" said Aeneas Briggs, rushing to Nick's side as soon as he was released. "I'll see to it that you get a football scholarship to the finest state college in the land!"

"But," said Nick, "I don't know how to play football. . . ."

"You can learn, you can learn. Here, let me help you pick up these clothes. Your parents will be worried about you. I shall drive you home. This has been a terrible experience. . . ."

"Well," said Nick, "it's an ill wind that blows no good."

"Come, come," said the Banker. "No time for philosophy."

"STOP! STOP!" cried a voice familiar to our hero from the far end of the platform. "I'VE GOT YOUR MAN!"

Nick turned and saw the fat detective hurrying toward them, the blond imposter handcuffed to his wrist. In his other hand the detective had the straw suitcase.

"Oh no," said our hero, whose feelings I need not describe.

"What in the deuce is this?" growled Chief Sheibly.

"I've got to go home, now," said Nick. "I hear my mother calling."

"So do I," said Aeneas Briggs. "Come along, my boy . . ."

"Nobody's going nowhere," said the Chief, "until I . . ."

"Got him with the goods, son," said the railroad detective, puffing up to Nick. "Here's the bag, and here's the bird. Found him hiding in the female washroom. I think he's a pervert. . . ."

"Great Scott!" cried Mr. Briggs. "Do you know who that is?"

"Yeh," said the detective, with a frown. "Some kind of per . . ."

"Pervert, my foot! That's Digby Pitt, the Eccentric Billionaire!"

"Hello, Aeneas," said that quixotic individual, to the consternation of our hero.

"*What the blazes is going on?*" cried the choleric Chief of Police.

"Well, well," said the railroad detective. "If it isn't Chief Sheibly and his boys. Good timing, Chief. I guess that takes care of the old adage about cops being around only when you don't want them." He handed the straw suitcase to Nick, who set it quickly down. "I imagine this young fellow will want to press charges, whoever this crook is, billionaire or no. . . ."

"I? Not I! I never saw that man before in my life," said Nick.

"Will somebody please explain . . . ?" cried Chief Sheibly.

"Now just a minute," said the detective, his color rising. "Isn't that your bag?"

"I never saw *it* before in my life, either," said Nick. "Listen, I've got to be going. It's after my bedtime. Early to bed and . . ."

"Wait!" cried Squire Farley, stepping forward. "That's the bag! Cheap straw suitcase. He uses them every time. Just ask my boy."

"Now we're getting somewhere," said Chief Sheibly.

"What's going on here?" asked the railroad detective.

"Open that bag, boys," ordered the Chief, and in a matter of moments the lid flew up, revealing tightly packed bundles of currency.

"Holy Cow!" cried one of the policemen. "A fortune!"

"What the blazes . . . !" exclaimed the detective.

"Ha ha ha ha ha!" laughed Digby Pitt. "It's worthless, absolutely worthless. Counterfeit, every last crisp brand-new bill of it. Look!" He held out a tastefully engraved portrait of Benjamin Franklin, tinted a pale shade of bilious green, which made the Sage appear to be suffering from a nauseous indisposition. "See what happens when you wash one off?"

With a gargling cry, Aeneas Briggs fell on his knees and ripped open one of the packets of hundred-dollar bills. "Swindled!" he cried.

"On your feet, Briggs!" barked Chief Sheibly, producing a pair of handcuffs. "That stuff belongs to the State of California, now!"

"I . . . I don't want it!" cried the Banker, struggling to his feet. "It's not mine! I'm being framed! Call my lawyer!"

"You'll have your day in court," growled Chief Sheibly as he chained the Banker's wrists behind him. "Now, what about this bozo?" he asked, pointing to the gentleman recently identified as Digby Pitt, the Eccentric Billionaire. "How does he fit in?"

"I wish somebody would tell *me*, Fred," said the detective, mopping his brow with a bandanna handkerchief. "I thought he stole this kid's suitcase. At least that's what the kid told me. . . ."

"I can explain," said Digby Pitt. "This boy was seated next to me on the train, and after some polite conversation, he fell asleep. It presently became necessary for me to heed nature's call, and noticing that the bag was fastened to his wrist, and therefore must contain something of value, I severed the chain with a pair of snips I carry with me at all times, one of my many eccentricities. . . ."

"Aha!" cried the detective. "You admit it, then!"

"I have nothing to hide," said Mr. Pitt. "I took the suitcase with me lest the boy and his valuables be parted by one of the many thieves who prowl the cars with impunity, despite the (ahem) efforts of the railroad to discourage them."

"A likely story," sneered the fat detective. "Why were you gone an hour or more? And what were you doing, hiding in the female terlet?"

"The train was crowded, and the gentlemen's rooms were all occupied. Nature's call having become urgent, I was forced to obey it to the best of my ability. Naturally, I was unwilling to be seen coming out of the ladies' room, once in. I knew that the boy was going all the way to Poco Lobo, where I was to get off also, planning to hire a car to take me to Santa Barbara, so I felt there was no hurry in that matter. I fell asleep, until I was rudely awakened by this well-intentioned but mistaken gentleman in the derby hat."

"How did you know there was bogus money in the suitcase?"

"To amuse myself and while away the time, I opened it. As the world knows, I am eccentrically fond of boys and interested in all their little affairs. I thought it would be a harmless entertainment to rummage through his boyish belongings. A moment's work with a hairpin found on the floor opened the cheap lock, but you can imagine my surprise when I looked inside! I immediately realized that the boy was running an errand for his employer, and was about to shut the suitcase when I noticed something wrong with one of the bills—being somewhat of an expert in money matters. I examined it, and saw immediately that it was a bungled counterfeit note, the ink coming off on my fingers. A hasty examination revealed that the suitcase was filled with counterfeit money, in uniform denominations of . . ."

"A likely story!" sneered Banker Briggs. "It's the old pigeon drop, Chief Sheibly. Arrest that man!"

"Ridiculous," said Digby Pitt with a laugh. "What would I, a billionaire twice over, want with your paltry half-million or so?"

"Chief Sheibly!" cried the banker. "I insist that you do your duty!"

"I intend to," said the Chief. "I'm taking you *all* in. We'll get this thing straightened out if it takes the rest of the night!"

"I am entirely innocent of any wrongdoing," said Nick, stoutly. "I shall gladly come along of my own accord. The American system of justice will clear me of all charges. I shall be vindicated."

"Boy, have I heard that song before," said one of the policemen.

"I have nothing to hide," said Nick.

"We'll check on *that*, too," said Chief Sheibly. "I intend to get to the bottom of things—fast!"

We shall spare our young readers the painful sequence of events which followed at the police station, and rejoin our hero the following day in a remote section of that establishment, as he lay in coarse prison garb in his cell, making himself as comfortable as possible on the single plank which served him as bed, and, as it were, board, being the only article of furniture provided save for a dirty slop bucket in a far corner. He was interrupted in his reverie by Mr. Briggs.

"Nicholas, my boy," said his employer, peering through the bars, "I'm leaving you now, free on bail, but I shall not forget you, never fear. Aeneas Briggs may have his faults, but disloyalty to faithful employees is not one of them. As soon as my lawyer arrives from New York City, we shall go to work and get a change of venue. There's a judge in Las Plugas, Cecil S. Poole, a classmate and fraternity brother of mine. We'll turn the tables on that rascal, Farley, yet!"

"What about Mr. Alibi," asked Nick, "and the half-a-million?"

"Flown the coop," said the Banker, making fluttering motions with his hands, "But there's no profit in crying over spilt milk. That's water under the bridge, my boy. The bird we want is that traitor, Farley." The banker laughed bitterly. "I can't wait to see his face when he's sitting right where you are now. Heh heh heh heh heh."

"Heh heh heh heh," laughed Nick. "Is there any chance of my getting out on bail, also?"

"I have spoken to your parents about that, my boy. They send their regards, by the way. I have advised strongly against it. You are much safer where you are. Much evil is afoot. My enemies have the upper hand, and will stop at nothing. I should never forgive myself

if anything happened to you. Your testimony is vital to
our case." The banker stuck his hand through the bars.
"Trust in me, my boy. You won't be here long. Naturally,
I shall keep you on my payroll until all this is over, at
half your regular wages, the money to be deposited in
your account which your father opened in his name. I
couldn't do less."

"God bless you, sir," said Nick, gratefully kissing his
employer's liver-spotted and bony but amazingly firm
hand. "I shall pray for you."

"That can't do any harm. My lawyer will visit you as
soon as he arrives. He will represent the both of us, a
considerable saving to you, by the way. He'll tell you
what to say, and you be sure to say it. Everything depends
on the both of us sticking to the same story. Consistency,
remember, is the hobgoblin of little minds, and most
juries are made up out of pinheads."

"You can count on me, sir."

"Good boy. You'll get that football scholarship, yet."

A week later, Nick was visited by Mr. E. Z. Blackstone III, of the prestigious firm of Blackstone, Blackstone, Scharfwitz & McFee, 10 Wall Street, New York
City. Mr. Blackstone had a commanding presence, being
dressed in a silk hat and tails. When he removed his top-
hat, the lawyer revealed a skull that was hairless as an
egg and shone as if polished with wax, which it was,
being a useful device for distracting hostile witnesses.

"This is the story, son," he said, having dusted off
Nick's board with a silk handkerchief before sitting

down: "We're claiming that you and Briggs have been the victims of a swindle cooked up by Farley to recoup his fortunes by default. Briggs held a note which he was going to call in on account of Farley's bad business practices, but Farley claimed he was able to pay off the loan in full, with money he had just inherited from his aunt in Long Beach, but because he had a lot of creditors, the deal had to be carried out in great secrecy. So you were told to go to Long Beach and pick up a suitcase with the money in it, which you did, only Farley had filled it with queer, working in league with that fink, Alibi, who was running a gambling parlor in the back room of the Charity Bazaar in cahoots with our boy, Farley. When you got back to Poco Lobo, he blew the whistle on Briggs, only we're going to fix *him*, but good. That's the story, son. Tight as an old maid's reticule."

"Where is Mr. Alibi?" asked Nick.

"In Costa Rica, for all I know. Forget him," said Mr. Blackstone. "Farley's all we need, and we got *him*, and how!"

"What will . . . happen to him?"

"Ten years maximum. Former pillar of the community, et cetera."

"Poor Frank," said Nick. "He won't put on many airs after this."

"As an accessory after the fact, the kid'll most likely end up in reform school. Do the brat a world of good. A sound thrashing every now and then never did a growing boy any harm."

"Heh heh heh heh," chuckled Nick. "When do we go to trial?"

"Well, we've got to get the venue changed, and that takes time. Be patient, son. Your folks sent you this." Mr. Blackstone opened his briefcase and took out a mason jar filled with water gruel. "Naturally, they'd like to come visit you, but we think it's a good idea for them to see you for the first time when you come to trial. You'll be pale and wan and that'll make your old . . . make your mother cry. Very effective on a jury."

"Whatever you say, sir," said Nick. "But it's lonely here."

"Maybe," said Mr. Blackstone, "but it's better than having a cellmate, considering the alternative."

"And what is that?" asked our hero, baffled.

"If you have to ask," said the lawyer, "you don't want to know."

After Mr. Blackstone had departed, Nick returned to his board and made a quick meal of his water gruel, which was a welcome change from the coarse prison fare, even if its taste was altered for the worse by a rusty file which had thoughtfully been placed inside the jar.

"What's that you've got there, son?" asked the jailer, who happened to be passing Nick's cell as he examined the implement in question.

"A cinnamon stick, sir," said our resourceful hero.

"Is that right?" asked the jailer, taking out his keys. "From where I'm standing it looks like a workout with the hose."

CHAPTER XII

A Daniel
Come to Judgment

☞

I shall spare my young readers the details of what our hero was not spared, and likewise speed over the succeeding months during which Aeneas Briggs managed to get his change of venue by claiming the impossibility of obtaining a fair trial in Poco Lobo, where a jury of his peers was sure to include a number in debt to the accused. The venue was therefore transferred to Las Plugas, as was our hero, who was placed in the only available cell in the crowded jailhouse, a compartment generally reserved for rabid dogs, hence measuring four feet by four feet, and illuminated by what feeble rays of light managed to filter through a peephole in the iron door.

Las Plugas was a favored location for changes of venue

throughout the area, and several more months of delay
followed, during which the tedium of Nick's confinement was relieved by the arrival of a daily ration of
tepid water and coarse black bread, spiced by the visits
of the jailhouse chaplain, a Seventh-Day Adventist who
diverted our hero by discussing his recent conversion
from the Mormon faith. Once a week, moreover, the
jailer informed Nick of the scores of the Stanford and
University of California football games, as he was required to do by law.

Many another boy might have lost hope and even
his mind under these conditions, our hero not having
heard from his family, his employer, or even his lawyer
since his removal from Poco Lobo. But Nick not only
kept his faith, but managed to preserve his naturally
resilient spirits by reciting to himself what scraps of
literature he could recall, including Demosthenes' *Ora-
tions,* the Pledge of Allegiance, the first stanza of the
National Anthem, five verses of *Snow-Bound,* the Boy
Scout Oath, Kipling's *If,* the opening lines of *The
Heathen Chinee* (the first poem he had ever learned by
heart), and the warning label on the can of Drano
kept in the bathroom at home. By nature a solitary lad,
Nick was better suited than most to confinement, and
by means of certain ingenious postures, he got in a bit
of exercise from time to time.

Still, he was glad to receive news one day that he had
a visitor, who turned out to be none other than Mr. E.
Z. Blackstone III.

"Well, well," he said, as he joined Nick in his cell. "Snug little place you have here."

"Thank you, sir," said Nick. "Where have you been?"

"Listen, son," said the lawyer. "I've been busier than a feather merchant at plucking time. Where's the light switch in here?"

"There isn't any," said Nick. "Couldn't you get my cell changed?"

"No need, no need," said Mr. Blackstone. "You'll be out of here before you know it."

"I'm certainly glad to hear that," said our hero.

"Sure. Now, I've got an appointment with the D.A., so I can't stay long, much as I'd like to, but I wanted to bring you up to date. I've got some bad news and some good news, and I'm going to give you the bad news first. Poole won't go along with our story. Farley's bound to appeal, and there's been too much publicity already, which increases the risk. The papers have had a field day with us, on account of the Teapot Dome stink. So, no tricks. That's the bad news."

"It certainly is," said Nick. "What's the good news?"

"The good news is we've found Alibi. He's in prison in Acapulco for attempting to bribe a customs officer. We don't have to worry about him for at least ten years, so he's gonna be the patsy, now. We can fix things so it looks like he was running the gambling operation without Briggs's knowledge, using the bazaar for a front. We've dug up some other dirt, too, with Farley's help. . . ."

"*Squire* Farley?"

"Yeh. Alphonse. He's with *us,* now. Briggs renewed his note and hired that brat of his again. Listen, we've got this thing sewed up tighter than your grandmother's Thanksgiving turkey. Of course, it's cost the old man a pile of dough. . . ."

"What about the half-a-million in counterfeit money. Won't . . . ?"

"That's where you come in, son. Briggs will maintain that he had been accumulating the stuff on the q.t. as evidence against Alibi, who had been slipping queer into the take from the bazaar. You found the money in Briggs's closet and thought it was the McCoy, only after you got to Cucamonga, you had a change of heart. . . ."

"But . . ."

"Look, son, I haven't got much time, so please don't interrupt me. You had a change of heart, and called Briggs, who arranged to meet you at the station with Chief Sheibly, who'll go along with us, too. Nobody'll believe that whacko billionaire, whose got more loose screws than Carter's has pills, and as soon as we can run down the railroad bull, we'll pay *his* price, and our worries will be over."

"But . . ."

"I know what you're thinking, son, but don't worry. The change-of-heart routine makes you technically almost the same as innocent!"

"But I *am* innocent!" cried Nick.

"Sure, we all were once upon a time, but that's life,

son. The point is, if you'll take a dive, which is legal
language for copping a plea, Poole will let you off easy.
The most you'll get is five years, maybe even less. . . ."

"Five years in prison!"

"That's another break. Because of your age, you'll get
sent to reform school. . . ."

"But they *beat* people there! You told me so yourself . . . !"

"Only with a belt these days. They outlawed baseball
bats two years ago. Believe me, it's better than prison,
considering the alternative. . . ."

"But why not blame the whole thing on Mr. Alibi?
Why do I have to be involved at all?"

"We thought about that, son. We tried to get the
D.A. to go along with 'unwitting participation,' see? But
it was no good. He wants some real meat, after all this
adverse publicity, and Poole backed him up. Don't forget, it's an election year."

"But can't you use Mr. Alibi for the real meat?"

"Sure, but that would mean extraditing him, and
that's running a big risk. He's a sharp cooky, and we'd
probably all end up in the clink. Listen, son, the important thing here is to protect the old man. Where's
your sense of gratitude? Where would you be today if
it hadn't been for Mr. Briggs?"

"I hadn't thought of it in that way."

"Right. So how about it? Help us protect the old man?"

"Five years," said Nick, "is a great deal of gratitude."

"Is that any way to talk? What's the rising generation

coming to? Listen, son, you may not know it, but the entire economic community is suffering from this thing. There's talk of a crash. The loss of confidence has been felt on Wall Street, and Bryan is shooting his mouth off about the Gold Standard again. If Briggs goes, the whole country will go, right down the drain. Where's your patriotism? Besides, I'm authorized to offer you ten thousand bucks and a football scholarship. You can learn the game while you're up the river."

"But what about my good name? I'm a Noxin, after all."

"You drive a hard bargain, son. I'll throw in a couple extra thou for your good name, but that's the most I can go. The old man is almost to the wall, and after he pays my fees, he'll be flatter than a honeymoon soufflé. Now, how about it?"

"How do I know I'll get the money?"

"How does anybody know anything? Look, son, you're dealing with two men from the world of business. Do you know what makes that world turn round?"

"Money?"

"What's *money?* Pieces of paper, hunks of metal. Without one thing they'd be worthless, and that one thing is printed right on every single blessed bill and coin. . . ."

"The U.S. Treasury?"

"*Trust,* son. Good old-fashioned trust. We're gonna trust in you, and you gotta trust in us. Listen, do you think the old man would go back on a promise to a loyal employee? You take care of him and he'll see to it that you get taken care of good and proper. That's the kind of old gentleman *he* is. When they made *him,* they broke the mold and threw it away. They don't make 'em like that anymore."

"Supposing I don't go along with it?"

"We'll bury you."

"Well," said Nick. "I guess I don't have much choice."

"That's the spirit, son! The reformatory isn't all that bad these days, they say. Got window curtains now and hot-water baths once a week, I hear. Craftshops, too, where you can earn a little spending money while learning an honorable trade, and you get to work outdoors in the fields after the first year."

"Picking beans?"

"If you want. Heck, the experience will do you good. Some people pay *money* to send their kids to military academies. What's the diff?"

"I never looked at it that way," said Nick.

"Sure. Listen, you behave yourself up there and they'll make you a trusty, and then you can beat the *other* kids with a belt. No matter how you look at it, son, America is the land of opportunity. By this time tomorrow, you'll be out of this hole and on your way!" Mr. Blackstone pounded on the door to be let out.

"Well," said Nick, "that's something."

"Right," said the lawyer, crawling out of the cell. "See you in court, son. Get a good night's rest."

Because of his daily exercise, our hero was able to walk into the courtroom with almost no assistance, though somewhat hampered by the chains on his wrists and ankles. As he entered the crowded hall of justice, Nick searched the faces of the spectators, looking for his family, but without success. There was one man half-hidden behind a pillar near the back of the courtroom who did bear a certain resemblance to his father, only Mr. Noxin did not customarily wear smoked lenses and certainly did not have a bushy black beard.

Painfully present, however, was Nick Noxin's nemesis, Frank Farley, who signaled his presence by placing his thumb to his nose and waggling his fingers at our hero, who responded to the rude greeting with the silent contempt it deserved, and marched to the defendants' table with as much dignity as he could muster. There he was greeted by Aeneas Briggs, who seemed the very picture of radiant good health, having spent the intervening months under a *nom de plaisir* at Corona Del Mar. Leaning forward with a smile, the Banker whispered a few words of encouragement. "Believe me, my boy," he said, "this is the best thing. It will restore the confidence of the community in our economic institutions. You will be a hero in banking history."

"You can trust me, sir," said Nick.

"Speaking of which," said Mr. Blackstone, whispering in his other ear as he held out a sheaf of papers. "There have been a few changes since I saw you last. We couldn't find the railroad bull, so the D.A. wouldn't go along with us at the last minute, but we've worked out something even better. . . ."

"What is that, sir?" asked Nick.

"Shh! shh!" hushed the lawyer, as the cry of "Oyez! Oyez!" heralded the arrival of Judge Cecil S. Poole, all rising as that eminence entered slowly from chambers, his gait determined as much by advanced age as by his size, which was substantial, his corpulence accentuated rather than concealed by his flowing robes. The Judge's countenance was of a purplish cast, highlighted by numerous veins in his cheeks, and his head somewhat resembled the plum native to California, if that fruit sported tufts of native cotton here and there around its stem.

Judge Poole's appearance did not decrease Nick's uneasiness over what Mr. Blackstone had told him, nor did the subsequent announcement of the charges to be placed against him, which was made by the prosecutor, a baker-kneed little man whose chief feature was the lack of a noticeable chin.

"The State of California," he declared in an offensive whine, "wishes to drop all charges against the Honorable Aeneas Briggs, said Briggs having been the dupe of unscrupulous employees, namely one B. Franklin (alias "Scarface," alias "Squint") Alibi, present whereabouts unknown, and Nicholas (alias "Nick," alias "Grocersboy," alias "Nick the Picker," alias "Sticky Nick") Noxin, seated before the bar. In league with the aforementioned Alibi, who, unbeknownst to the Honorable Aeneas Briggs, was operating a gambling den in the back room of the Honorable Briggs's Charity Bazaar, the aforementioned Noxin did conspire, connive, and in all ways conceive a plot to bilk his employer out of a cool half-million bucks. Uh, dollars."

"What in the . . . ?" exclaimed Nick to Mr. Black-stone.

"I told you there'd been a few changes, son. Don't worry, it'll all work out. . . ."

"SILENCE IN THE COURT!" bellowed Judge Poole, accompanying his remarks with a blow from his gavel.

"Moreover," continued the District Attorney, "the aforementioned Alibi did, according to evidence now in our hands," here waving a sheaf of papers, "engage in numerous other enterprises of a nature too loathsome to mention in mixed company, and in these activities, which soiled the pure sands of our own Bragadura Cove, he was aided and abetted and in all ways assisted by the aforementioned Noxin, who enlisted his aid with full knowledge aforethought of the heinous nature of Alibi's activities, which included the illegal importation of aliens into this great and wonderful state, undesirable representatives of the Yellow Peril which were palmed off onto the unsuspecting the Honorable Alphonse Farley as Mexican nationals, causing his agricultural enterprise to fail, resulting in considerable tax loss to his community. Mr. Farley has indicated his willingness to testify on the State's behalf, and his son, Fauntleroy Farley, Esq., will bear witness against the accused, also, testifying as to his detestable character—Your Honor's permission forthcoming, for he is but a boy in his teens. . . ."

"Permission granted," mumbled the Judge.

"Thank you, Your Honor . . . as will the Honorable Aeneas Briggs, once the charges have officially been erased from the record, allowing him to return to his former position of civic responsibility and esteem, the stain removed from his sterling reputation and his good name returned to him forever and ever."

"Amen!" said Banker Briggs in a hoarse whisper.

"Your Honor," said Nick, rising with a clank of chains. "I have a statement to make at this time. . . ." Our hero was not, I hasten to add, unfamiliar with courtroom procedure, having acquainted himself with the exciting contents of the broken set of California Court Records which made up a large percentage of his father's library.

"WHAT?" roared the judge.

Lawyer Blackstone now rose, pushing Nick back into his seat. "Your Honor, my client wishes . . . ow!"

Biting the hand that held him, Nick clanked to his feet again. "Your Honor!" he cried. "I object!"

"SILENCE!" roared the Judge, pounding his gavel until splinters flew. "I will allow no irregularities in my courtroom! Children must be seen and not heard!"

"Your Honor," said Mr. Blackstone, taking hold of our hero's neck in a quick hammerlock, "I should like to apologize for the behavior of my client, who is a misguided youth, suffering from the influence of evil companions . . . oof!"

"Your Honor!" cried Nick, having broken the lawyer's grip with a well-placed blow from his elbow, "I object! I am innocent of all charges!"

"SHUT UP, YOU MISERABLE PUNK!" bellowed the Judge, his face a colorful mixture of magenta and cobalt blue, not unlike the native sunsets of his glorious state. "If there's any objecting to be done around here, it should be by the outraged citizenry of this community. I shouldn't be surprised if a few real men take matters into their own hands once the full details of your crimes are known, and the members of the press here present may quote me, providing my remarks are on the front page of the early afternoon editions!"

"But, Your Honor!" cried our hero, struggling against the combined forces of his lawyer and his employer. "I've got . . ."

"You've got five years additional for contempt of court!" cried the Judge, pounding his gavel until the handle broke. "Bailiff, bind and gag the prisoner! Let's get this show on the road!"

"STOP! STOP IN THE NAME OF THE LAW!"

This command from the back of the courtroom brought everyone's head around, save for that of our hero, who was hampered by the bailiff's foot, which was on his neck. This impediment was soon removed, however, as down the aisle came Mr. Q. Digby Pitt, Mr. B. Franklin Alibi, the railroad detective, and the Governor of the State of California.

"A grave injustice is being perpetrated here," said Mr. Digby Pitt, who had not been idle since our hero saw him last.

"Put everyone except the spectators under lock and key!" ordered the Governor. "We're going to clear up this mess, or this isn't an election year!"

CHAPTER XIII

Free
and Clear!

☛

"You see," said Mr. Pitt to our hero, when they were alone at last in a clean, well-lighted cell, "I refused to believe that I could have been wrong in my assessment of your character, despite appearances to the contrary. I therefore hired the services of the railroad detective, Mr. Horace Bubb, who undertook for me a private investigation of the nefarious activities of Aeneas Briggs. These led him to Mr. Alibi, who, while incarcerated in Mexico for attempting to practice medicine without a license, had been brought back into the arms of his parents' religion by the entreaties of one of its representatives, who happened to be sharing his cell. Repenting of his past life of crime, Mr. Alibi was eager to help us in our good work, and will testify against Briggs, in return for which he will be granted immunity from prosecution.

"Mr. Alibi was easily persuaded by me that you were involved in Briggs's network of crime quite unwittingly. We have likewise convinced the Attorney General of your inadvertent complicity, and, if you cooperate, you also will be granted immunity."

"I shall be glad to do what I can," said our hero, "to guarantee that justice will be done."

"As a further reward for your cooperation in removing this stain from the gleaming face of American enterprise, thus restoring the shaken faith of the community in our institutions, I am prepared to offer you a responsible position in one of my numerous firms, upon your graduation from the university of your choice."

"Oh thank you, sir!" cried our hero, kissing the hand of the man he once thought to be an imposter. "You will not be sorry!"

Let us not tarry, young reader, over the details of the criminal proceedings brought against Poole, Briggs, Farley, Farley, and Blackstone, who were sentenced to a total of 1500 years at hard labor in the various penal institutions of the enlightened state of California, during the course of which the crooked judge dropped dead from apoplexy, Squire Farley lost his mind, Aeneas Briggs his fortune, and E. Z. Blackstone's head its shine.

Let us instead hasten to the final day of that trial, and the moment of our hero's triumph. Sentences had al-

ready been pronounced on the culprits by the Honorable
Douglas N. Lincoln, a retired State Supreme Court
Justice appointed by the Governor for that purpose,
each separate sentence followed by applause from the
crowded galleries and music from the assembled members of the Poco Lobo Marching Marine Band, the
venue having been returned to that worthy community.

Our hero, having played such an important role in the
trial, received quite a bit of attention in the public
prints, so much so that Mr. Noxin was able to make a
tidy profit by selling Nick's belongings as souvenirs,
replenishing them as needed from the Salvation Army
Store in Santa Barbara. It was decided, therefore, to
allow Nick a final display of his forensic abilities, which,
to the admiration of the spectators and the consternation
of the culprits—Frank Farley, especially—had stood him
in such good stead on the stand.

A platform had been especially constructed for that
purpose, which, when our hero mounted it by means of
a ladder, raised him to the level of the Judge, to whom
he addressed his opening remarks concerning the fitness
of the sentences to the crimes, and allowed him thereby
a suitable height from which to look down upon the
wretched prisoners before the bar as he lectured them
on their numerous transgressions against the people of
the great state of California, holding them out to the
Rising Generation as an example of the consequences of
Doing Bad, in the hope that the Youth of America would
strive to Do Good.

"And so," he concluded, as the prisoners were bundled
without ceremony out the back door, "we make use of
adversity, for if two wrongs do not make a right, it is an
ill wind that blows no good. And now," continued our
hero, with a modest gesture of self-deprecation, "a few
words concerning . . . ourself."

Having said this, Nick Noxin walked to the far end
of the platform and gazed down on the crowded courtroom. Many familiar faces were there, including that of
his benefactor, Mr. Pitt, and his instructor, Mr. Cosmo
Castle, who naturally wished to be present at the triumphant display of his prize pupil's abilities. But most
welcome of all to Nick were the beaming countenances
of his family, which he located easily this time by the
American flags being waved by his brothers, who were
dressed in sailor suits provided for the occasion by Mr.
Israel free of charge (as stated in block letters on the front
and back of each middy blouse). Mr. Noxin was decked
out in full Masonic regalia (48th Degree), and his wife
was dressed in her best Quaker finery, her plain black
cloth coat and modest white cotton shawl creating an
image of touching simplicity, not a little resembling
Whistler's immemorial portrait of his own beloved parent.

"What I am about to say," began Nick, "is addressed
particularly to the citizens of this wonderful community,
so let me begin by saying 'My Fellow Americans,' or better yet, just plain . . . folks."

Allowing himself a shy smile, Nick looked down at his
feet. "For I am but a poor boy born of humble people,

much like yourselves, who know the value of a dollar well earned in honorable, hard-working toil, and it is to you I speak, my fellow citizens, of work and wage. We are the many whose efforts and integrity provide the energy and the bulwarks of this great nation, and it is from us that the grave figure of Justice behind me derives his awesome powers, symbolized by his otherwise empty robes. . . ."

Nick turned and pointed to Judge Lincoln, whose craggy features involuntarily rippled with what seemed, from a distance, to be a smile of acknowledgment.

"Folks," continued Nick, solemnly, "I want to take this opportunity to set the record straight for once and for all. Despite the fact that I have been granted complete and total immunity from prosecution for my unwitting complicity in the acts for which the prisoners will pay the just penalties accorded them by due process, despite that fact, I say, vile slanders, calumnies, innuendoes, and smears continue to be aimed at me, both in private and in public places. Only today, in the washroom of this temple of justice, I saw an egregious smear against my name, which I shall not dignify by repetition.

"Let there be no mistake, my fellow folks, these slurs and slimy innuendoes are undoubtedly well-meaning, the scurrilous work of those few who would set themselves up above the law so as to rectify what they conceive to be a wrong, much as the public prints dragged my name throught the mud some months ago, an act of unforgivable presumption which I am willing to forgive and forget once the lawsuit I have initiated runs its course.

"If only my name were involved, if only 'Nick Noxin' was being daubed with well-intentioned slime, I would not care, but these slanders and unfounded accusations, this foul gossip and filthy rumor in the name of 'truth,' also involve the name and the honor of my dear family, who are present here today, besmirched with the muck of those foul, though well-meant, attacks. My wonderful, careworn old mother in her plain cloth coat, and my hardworking, honest old father in his distinguished fraternal robes. My three talented, industrious brothers, Obie, Hardy, and little Knox . . . these have all suffered with me these attacks on the Noxin name, which remain as stains on the sacred tablets of the Bill of Rights and have even soiled the sanctity of the First Amendment. . . ."

Nick paused and gave a slow shake to his dark, thoughtful head, then smiled sadly. "But we bear no grudges, hold no malice. We Noxins will go on, smeared and besmirched, with heads held high. We will survive, and not merely survive, but persist, for we, like yourselves, folks, are representative of those humble many who make America great, those silent millions who in their quiet hearts keep the faith."

Here Nick choked a bit, as did several others in the courtroom, and one man, thought to be Mr. J. Adams Quincy, Nick's Grammar School Principal, was seen to depart out the door, a handkerchief pressed to his mouth.

"And if it were only my name and the name of my dear family that were at stake, I should not honor these foul, well-meant slanders by alluding to them. But as they stain us, so they stain you, my fellow humble Americans, and as they stain you, so are they so much slime hurled in the very face of all we hold precious. Even worse," said Nick, after a long pause to let the meaning of his words sink in, "in that these attacks question the immunity which I have enjoyed from persecution, immunity given to me by a duly constituted representative of the American system of justice" (here pointing to Judge Lincoln) "then, my fellow Americans, they are aimed at the freedoms we all enjoy and which make our wonderful way of life possible.

"Therefore," continued Nick, "I have decided to take steps to put an end to these vile slanders, however well-meaning they may be, by standing before you today, and declaring once and for all, forthrightly and openly, that I am indeed responsible for unwitting complicity in an act that has been judged criminal by those duly constituted to make that decision. . . ."

Here Nick was forced to hold up his hand for quiet. "But before you jump to hasty conclusions, my fellow friends, let me explain further the nature and implications of that unwitting complicity. For I do not merely admit responsibility for that complicity, I cherish it. I wrap myself in it as with the American flag, one nation,

invisible. . . . But you know those words, folks, so dear
to every American schoolboy's heart. The important thing
is *why* I was unwittingly involved in a criminal act without my knowledge, and that was, my fellow citizens, because I was carrying out my employer's duly constituted
instructions! Loyalty, folks, simple, unadulterated, good
old-fashioned American loyalty was the reason!"

Here Nick provided an interlude by turning and
smartly saluting the flag by the bench, which bore the
emblem of the proud Bear State.

"Were we," he went on after the applause had died,
"were any and all of us, to question the duly constituted
authority of our employers, to refuse to carry out instructions sanctioned by that authority, behind which—as a
boy not unfamiliar with the law I can assure you—behind
which stands the Constitution itself and its duly constituted representative, the President of the United States,
His Excellency, Calvin Coolidge (who was on the telephone to me just this morning, expressing his regrets that
he could not be here today), what would happen? Let me
explain to you carefully what would happen, my fellow
hardworking Americans. The mighty wheels of industry
would grind to a halt, and the number one nation in the
world, under God, would be a smoking ruin overnight.
Let me explain that in simpler terms, humble folks. The
plain fact of it is that you would all, every one of you,
be out of a job tomorrow!"

Nick punctuated each word by striking his fist into his

open palm, and was again forced to hold up his hand to calm the ensuing confusion, relaxing his frown into a smile of reassurance.

"Up until this moment, my fellow Americans, I have not used the word 'guilty' in describing my unwitting complicity, but I want to use that word now, and with tones of pride. For you see, folks," said Nick, his voice deep with sincerity and his youthful jowls resonant with earnest purpose, "I *am* guilty, guilty of abiding faith in the American system of free enterprise, which is built on the bedrock of trust, the very basis of our prosperity— unequaled, let me add, anywhere in the world—which is now under attack by those well-meaning, godless fault-finders who have hurled their vile filth at *us,* by which I mean not only I, and my family, but all you fine, decent, upstanding folks seated before me. Yes, I *am* guilty, guilty as charged, and I know that you are all guilty, too, for it is guilt like ours that has made America what it is today!"

Raising his hands in the familiar sign of benediction, Nick smiled down at the good people of Poco Lobo, as the Marine Band softly played the opening bars of the "Battle Hymn of the Republic." "In conclusion, folks, what has here today been established beyond a shadow of a doubt, thanks to the integrity of the American system of jurisprudence, is my complete and total vindication. For I am guilty of being *innocent,* innocent of any reserva-tions, any suspicions, any glimmer of doubt or fault-finding concerning the soundness of the economic foundations of our great republic, with liberty and justice for all, forever endeavor . . . Amen!"

As Nick dropped his hands, the Marine Band swung into the rousing chorus of the grand old hymn, and three American flags were seen sailing through the air, along with a number of hats, shawls, Masonic emblems, and a baby. Placards appeared here and there reading "NOXIN NOW!"—for, despite his tender years, our hero had been mentioned in the Poco Lobo *Howler* as a possible candidate for office—and a cannon in the town square was fired off, the reverberations shaking the walls of the temple of justice, which continued to shake after the echo had died, as above the sound of the band could be heard a distant rumble, like thunder, and then the platform on which our hero was standing began to sway and the windows of the courtroom to rattle, as a portrait of Abraham Lincoln fell from the wall behind the Judge who shared his name if not his political affiliation.

Those of my young readers who are familiar with the often violent history of California are aware that the rumbling and rattling were not caused by the band, the cannon, or the wild applause occasioned by our hero's triumphant speech, but resulted from one of those periodic tremors which shake the Pacific Slope from its usual repose, the most famous of which had caused the destruction by fire of San Francisco some twenty years previous to the time of our story. Though hardly of the force of that disastrous earthquake, the tremors felt in Poco Lobo

that day did wreak considerable damage to nearby Santa
Barbara, and were of sufficient strength to destroy a number of older buildings in the smaller township as well,
including Mr. Briggs's brick bank and the courthouse itself, a venerable and historic structure built rather hastily
by the founding fathers of Poco Lobo some fifty years
earlier, so as to accommodate the numerous litigations
attendant upon the establishment of a frontier community.

Built of stone, the courthouse was designed on the
classical principle of post-and-lintel construction, an antique system of balances which, though functionally adequate under normal strain, and beautiful to behold in its
simplicity and purity of line, was unable to withstand the
lateral thrust of an earthquake, and collapsed suddenly
inward after the first tremor had climaxed the remarks of
our hero, thus catching the occupants of the building unaware, and burying them all under tons of rubble. Only
Nick Noxin survived, having been catapulted out an open
window by the swaying of his supple platform, and by
one of those miracles which often attend such cataclysmic
upheavals of nature, he found himself lying in the street
outside the former chief landmark of Poco Lobo—now
just a pyramidal mound over which hung a sun-struck
cloud of dust.

Getting to his feet and brushing himself off, Nick regarded the ruin which had only moments before been
the scene of his greatest triumph, entertaining such mixed
emotions as my young readers may well imagine, having

survived not only his family and half the town, but his benefactor, Mr. Pitt, as well. Nick, however, was not unaware of his good fortune in being alive, and his gloomy reflections lasted for only a moment. He was at the point of offering humble thanks to his Creator, when a second tremor struck the town, of less force, but sufficient to open a chasm beneath Nick's feet into which he tumbled without a sound. As suddenly as it had opened, the chasm closed, leaving not a trace of our hero save a few footprints in the dust, nor was there a single witness to his departure.

When he regained his senses, Nick found himself in a dark, damp, foul-smelling space, and, for a brief moment, thought he was back in his cell in Las Plugas. As his recollection returned, he realized his error, and by feeling about with hands and feet (somehow his shoes had departed), Nick was able to determine that he was in a circular space, a sort of tunnel the function of which was defined by the noisome liquid that gurgled past where he was sitting. Through another *lusus naturae,* Nick had fallen into the Poco Lobo sewer system, which, though damaged by the earthquake, continued to function, having been designed with utility rather than beauty in mind. Instantly recalling his Boy Scout training, Nick followed the flow of the current, his progress sped by the contents of the reservoir that fed the Farley Farms irrigation system, which, released by the cataclysm, found their way through storm sewers into the main artery. Though his passage was often painful, it had the virtue of being swift, and in no time at all Nick found himself shot from the orifice at the far end of the sewer into the waters of Bragadura Cove, where a tidal wave raised by the quake threw him far up onto the shore, in the company of much flotsam and jetsam, including a whale, several sharks, a Japanese tuna boat, and a skeleton encased below the knees in a barnacle-covered block of cement.

Getting to his feet once again, and pausing only to brush the worst debris from the ragged remnants of his Palm-Beach suit, Nick set off down the beach with that purposeful gait so revelatory of his character. Having first encountered our barefoot boy in motion, let us now leave him in a similar condition, secure in the knowledge that no matter what his intended direction, Nick Noxin is surely

BOUND TO RISE!